Dear Readers,

Welcome to the clandestine alleys of "Emberglade," where mystery intertwines with suspense, and every turning page reveals a concealed truth. As the writer of this enigmatic world, I am both delighted and honoured to have you as a companion on this riveting journey.

Within these pages, you'll encounter characters draped in ambiguity, navigating a landscape where nothing is as it seems. "Emberglade" is a tapestry of secrets and uncertainties, where allies may wear the mask of adversaries, and every revelation deepens the mystery.

Pay attention to the ♦ breaks

These are scattered throughout the narrative. They are your silent guides, signalling critical junctures – whether a shift in scene or a change in perspective. Let them be your compass through the shadows and revelations.

In the heart of this chilling tale, where suspense is a palpable presence, trust your instincts, question the shadows, and brace yourself for the unforeseen. As you traverse the clandestine paths of "Emberglade," may the thrill captivate your senses, and the mysteries linger long after the final revelation.

Thank you for choosing to unravel the secrets of "Emberglade." Enjoy the suspense.

Warm regards,

Levi T Evans

Contents

Chapter 1... 1

Chapter 2... 10

Chapter 3... 20

Chapter 4... 28

Chapter 5... 38

Chapter 6... 43

Chapter 7... 49

Chapter 8... 56

Chapter 9... 66

Chapter 10... 78

Chapter 11... 83

Chapter 12... 91

Chapter 13... 98

Chapter 14... 110

Chapter 15... 117

Chapter 16... 121

Chapter 17... 128

Chapter 18... 135

Chapter 19... 142

Chapter 20... 150

Chapter 21... 156

Chapter 22... 161

Chapter 23... 166

Chapter 24... 173

Chapter 25... 178

Chapter 26... 185

Emberglade

CHAPTER 1

The shadowy figure before me seethed with rage, his eyes glowing like hot coals—nothing like the dad I once knew. For thirty-two years, he'd been a devoted, loving father who raised my sisters and me alongside Mum. Our home overflowed with laughter and joy. I even took on his name, and Grandma often said I had his deep brown eyes, wicked grin, and wavy black hair. Those were the good days, before the divorce shattered our happy family.

That's when everything changed. He changed.

Now he's with Layla, a woman twelve years his junior. She seems nice enough, but I can tell he resents her presence. I suspect he's not over Mum and never will be. Poor Layla has no idea she's just a replacement, a warm body to fill the void Mum left behind. Oh, and did I mention Layla came after Dad's short-lived affair that ended his marriage? Yeah, that fling barely lasted a few months before he latched onto Layla. But even so, it's obvious he still longs for Mum.

I'll never forget that night Dad showed up reeking of beer, wearing his usual "pub uniform" - a faded black t-shirt and worn trousers. The outfit he dons whenever he crawls into a bottle.

"Junior, I've always loved your mum. This wasn't supposed to happen," he slurred.

I often wonder what's going through his mind when he spouts nonsense like that. Does he really think he's absolved of blame? Is he trying to distance himself from the wreckage he created? Shifting responsibility? He's only fooling himself.

"Dad, you can't keep saying these things. Not when you've been with Layla over a year now," I replied, trying to pull him back to reality.

One look at his wounded eyes told me my words hit their mark, shutting him down. That night, I left him alone at the bar. I could no longer afford to be his emotional crutch. Work called early the next day, and I couldn't show up drained.

That was the last time I saw my dad.

As James Senior signalled the bartender for one last drink, he retreated into his thoughts. Like clockwork, he dragged himself to his usual corner - an isolated spot claimed by the same worn, brown stool each weekend. There he sat, observing the joy and companionship around him.

Once, his own life brimmed with laughter and smile-induced aches. Now relegated to the corner, he traced the scratches on the table before him.

"Pint of Stella for you," the bartender announced, sliding it over.

James rose wordlessly, leaving the full glass behind as he navigated the rowdy crowd and slipped outside.

The pub's convenience, just down the block, explained his near nightly visits. Some blamed it for the town's decline - a hangout for gangs and brawls so common ambulances and cop cars were routine. But that's just Emberglade. Best steer clear if you want to avoid regret. Locals called it "rough."

Stumbling home, James waved to his neighbour through the window before entering his unlocked house. He'd long stopped carrying keys, opting to hide one under the mat. Foolish, some said. What about Layla's safety? Didn't he care if someone just walked right in? Fortunately, it was only James coming home tonight.

Layla sat comfortably on the sofa, eyes glued to her favourite show. "Always watching that rubbish," James grumbled.

"A 'hello' would've been nice. How was your night?" Layla asked.

"Don't speak to me like that," James snapped, anger escalating.

"I'm just asking about your evening," she replied hesitantly.

In a burst of rage, James grabbed her hair, revealing an aggression Layla had never witnessed. He yanked hard, tearing out strands as she cried out. Wrapping both hands around her hair, he tightened his grip despite her pleas.

"You're hurting me! Let go!" Layla screamed.

James shoved her to the cold floor and reached for her throat. His slender fingers encircled her neck, squeezing as Layla gasped for air. She struggled in vain, her face purpling, voice fading.

Something in James shifted, and he released his grip. Layla gulped air but was too weak to flee. In one swift move, James pounced, forcing a half-eaten banana into her mouth while pressing her throat. Immobilised under his weight, she fought valiantly until she could fight no more. Her strength ebbed away. Her limbs grew heavy, and her head slumped to the floor.

The man she loved just strangled her to death.

James Senior drifted to sleep as if nothing had happened, not an ounce of remorse troubling his mind. The lifeless form sprawled on his living room floor went unnoticed. In an instant, he closed his eyes. When he opened them again, daylight flooded the room, and Layla's body came into focus. His gaze fell upon the shattered necklace around her neck - the one he'd given her as a symbol of eternal love and protection, a gift celebrating their anniversary. Now it lay broken, much like his promises and her life.

Reality sank in. The woman he'd built a life with, the one he cherished, was dead by his hands. Has he ever truly loved her? Or had his love consumed him? Could he not control himself? This man with the clean record, a father of three, now risked losing everything. His life careened down an unintended path, and he refused to let it spiral further.

Glancing at the black gloves on his hands, the gravity of the situation weighed on him. He couldn't walk away now. Gently gathering Layla's lifeless body, he carried her to the car and sped toward the nearest hospital.

Alarm gripped James. This wasn't his intent, not murder on this scale. Could he somehow evade the charges? Rushing Layla to the hospital seemed his only hope of saving himself and clinging to the last shreds of his humanity. Time pressed upon him as he raced ahead, knowing swift action was critical. His mind churned as he drove, grappling with the magnitude of his plight.

The once quiet drive now crackled with unbearable tension as he pulled into the hospital parking lot.

James parked haphazardly and leapt from the car, leaving Layla's lifeless body sprawled across the backseat. He sprinted toward the hospital entrance, mind swirling in a hurricane of panic.

Propelled by desperation and fear, James burst into the hospital, his hurried footsteps echoing his frenzied thoughts. Once inside, his panicked cries for help reverberated through the sterile corridors. This time, fortune smiled upon him as the pleas reached the ears of several doctors, who immediately sprang into action.

Their hurried footsteps echoed down the hall, keeping pace with his frenzied state of mind. Guilt and dread consumed James as he led them to the car, clinging to a faint sliver of hope that Layla could still be saved.

But when they arrived, the backseat was empty. Layla's body had vanished without a trace.

James spun around, confusion and shock etched on his face.

"She was right here! I don't understand..." His voice trailed off as the doctors exchanged bewildered looks. Where could she have gone? How was this possible?

Questions raced through James's mind. Had she regained consciousness and wandered off disoriented? Been forcibly taken? Or was something even more sinister at play? The uncertainty gnawed at him, his composure unravelling by the second under the harsh parking lot lights.

He glanced back towards the hospital, irrationally hoping this chilling nightmare would reverse itself. Turning back to the doctors, he stammered,

"I'm...I'm sorry. I thought she was here." His voice wavered, grasping for some logical explanation but unable to maintain his crumbling facade.

Leaving the hospital behind, James returned to his car, the weight of everything threatening to crush him. How would he explain Layla's disappearance? The police would surely get involved, trapping him further in his web of lies.

At home, his hands trembled as he dialled the police, pulse racing as he awaited an answer.

"Emberglade Police. Are you calling to report a crime?" the voice on the other end asked calmly.

James struggled to find words.

"Um, yes. I'm James Jones. I need to report a missing person - my girlfriend. I don't know where she is. I thought she'd be home, but she's gone. I can't reach her." His voice quivered with feigned fear and desperation.

"Please stay calm, sir. Protocol requires a twenty-four hour wait before filing a report. When did you last see her?"

"She said she was going out with friends," James lied, thoughts spinning as he improvised.

"I see. We'll need to wait twenty-four more hours to file a report. In the meantime, I urge you to contact her friends from that night. If she's still missing tomorrow, call us back. I'll note this for the next officer."

"O-okay, thanks," James stammered, hanging on the officer's every word.

"Of course. Let us know if any updates arise."

James spent the next agonising day home alone, curtains drawn, doors locked, anxiety mounting. He considered calling Layla's friends as advised but knew he couldn't. Contacting them would unravel everything. One more day - he just needed to wait one more day before calling the police again.

At dawn, James could wait no longer. Imagining a worried boyfriend would call immediately, he dialled, the familiar ring grating his nerves until someone finally answered.

"Emberglade Police. Reporting a crime?"

"Yes, I called yesterday about a missing woman. The officer made a note. Can you check?" James hurriedly explained.

"Let me access those notes... Ah yes, you reported a missing girlfriend and were asked to follow up today."

"That's right. She's still missing, and I'm really worried now," James lied, injecting escalating concern into his voice.

"I'll need your address to send officers right over," the dispatcher said, tone reassuring yet doing nothing to slow James's pounding heart. Soon the police would be at his door, questioning and scrutinising. His own home, the very crime scene, was about to be turned inside out.

As he awaited their arrival, anxiety mounted. His clammy hands trembled, pulse throbbing. A knock at the door made him jolt. He rushed to answer. The officers' presence, a stark reminder of the grim reality closing in on him.

Ushering them to the kitchen, James struggled to appear innocent, the act slipping through his fingers. The officers gently probed with calculated questions, gauging his every reaction. He felt their watchful stares, the suspicion in their eyes. His attempts to seem concerned and calm seemed feeble against their scrutiny.

Sitting across from them, the room grew heavy with tension, the air thickening. Their eyes tracked his every move, searching for deceit. James fought to stay composed, suppressing his inner turmoil. The walls closed in as his actions weighed down on him.

Meticulously, the officers extracted details on all of Layla's connections - addresses, numbers, workplaces. With each bit of intel James relinquished, he feared he was only further condemning himself.

Having gathered enough, the officers left with James' escort. From the window, he watched them methodically knock on neighbourhood doors. Silently, he prayed their inquiries wouldn't unearth anything substantial, that no one had seen or heard anything damning.

A week crawled by in agonising anticipation. Each day James anxiously awaited word from the police, only to be met with stony silence. Despite persistent calls for updates, they withheld all details, threatening to cite him for wasting resources. As James halfheartedly tried to resume his routine, a knock interrupted his idleness.

Two stern officers stood at his door. "Mister James Jones? I'm Senior Officer Bellis, this is Officer Humphries. We need to discuss your missing partner report. May we come in?" Bellis' tone left no room for debate. As they entered, tension swiftly choked the room, leaving James with an unshakable sense of peril.

"It's been over a week since anyone has seen or heard from Layla, James," one officer stated, voice neutral yet laced with suspicion.

James's heart hammered. They were closing in on him.

"Are you suggesting I killed my own girlfriend?" James erupted, words spewing forth in a mix of defiance and dread. He sensed their doubt, their belief in his guilt.

The pressure built as he knew he must choose his next words carefully.

"Did you murder her?" The blunt question hung in the air, laden with accusation. James's eyes flashed with anger and alarm. They were backing him into a corner, dissecting his every word and movement for cracks in his facade. Probing for the confession or slip-up that would confirm their suspicions.

"What are you talking about?" James snapped, voice wavering slightly as his pulse quickened. He felt desperation clawing at him, the need to divert their attention.

"They found her body, James. No one else had motive to kill her but you," one officer stated coldly, calculated to destabilise James's defences. It was the pivotal blow he'd dreaded, dropping on him like a ton of bricks. As the reality of Layla's death sank in, his heart plummeted.

"You're crazy! I loved her; there's no way she's dead! I don't believe you!" James yelled, with denial and anguish twisting together inside him. He clung to his claims in desperation, trying to convince them and himself that this nightmare wasn't real. But he could feel their skepticism, sensing the mounting evidence that could be found and used against him.

The officers exchanged a knowing look, subtle but clear. James's reactions had sealed his guilt in their minds. They'd reached a conclusion, the culmination of their investigation.

"James Lewis Jones, you're under arrest for the murder of Layla Smith." The words rang with chilling finality, shattering James's world. Suffocating panic gripped him as the severity of the charges crystallised. His mind raced wildly, grappling with the nightmare his actions had created.

CHAPTER 2

The savoury scent of bacon greeted me as I shuffled into the kitchen, still groggy from oversleeping. My family was already gathered around the table, nearly finished with breakfast.

"Well, well, look who decided to join us, James Jones Junior," my sister Shannon remarked sarcastically, using my full name and not even glancing up from her plate. She had always been the cocky one.

I shot her an irritated look as I slid into my usual seat.

"Hey, cut me some slack. I was out late with Dad last night. We don't get a lot of guy time these days."

My mum's expression soured at the mention of my dad. She aggressively stabbed at her omelette; the divorce had clearly left its mark. My sister Selena sat quietly, as always. Her brilliance made most people uneasy and reticent around her. As for me, I got saddled with the charm and good looks.

"Oversleeping again, huh?" Shannon smirked, laying it on thick.

"I'm sure calling in 'sick' went over great with your boss."

I bit my tongue, refusing to take the bait. Shannon had a knack for getting under my skin.

"Actually, my boss is really understanding, but you're right, I can't make a habit of it. I just want to take advantage of the time I get with Dad now." I replied evenly.

Mum's expression softened a bit, though her faint smile seemed tinged with sadness. Selena and I had moved on more easily; the divorce cut deeper scars for Shannon.

"Come join us," Mum urged as I shuffled into the kitchen, but my churning stomach protested breakfast after last night's revelry. I settled for just chatting with my family instead.

"This omelette is dreadful, Mum," Shannon grimaced dramatically after swallowing a rubbery bite.

"Clearly those cooking classes were a waste." She said with a smirk.

I shot her a warning look – leave it to Shannon to stir up trouble first thing in the morning.

"If you don't like my cooking, make your own breakfast," Mum fired back, annoyance flashing in her eyes.

"Selena is enjoying it, aren't you dear?"

Selena nodded enthusiastically, lips smacking on a piece of bacon.

"It's wonderful, Mum," she mumbled between bites.

Shannon rolled her eyes. "Arse-kisser," she muttered.

I chuckled under my breath. Classic Shannon, always looking to get a rise out of people. We both inherited that troublemaking streak from Dad, while Mum and Selena were much more even-tempered.

As Selena quietly finished up and took Shannon's plate to wash it, I marvelled at her perpetual kindness. At thirty, she was still single, which made me wonder if she was just too nice for most men. But then again, here I was at twenty-four, just as single as my older sister.

"Anyone up for a movie night this week?" Selena asked brightly, forever trying to unite our fractured family.

I loved my older sisters, though I preferred hanging out with friends. Selena's crippling shyness left her with few companions beyond us.

"Sorry, hon, my bowling tournament is this week," Mum replied.

I found her hobby embarrassing but never admitted it - I knew how much it meant to her.

"You guys are such losers," Shannon scoffed with a playful glint in her eyes. I shot her a gentle fake punch in retaliation.

"Says the thirty-year-old still living at home without a boyfriend," I volleyed teasingly.

"I'm an independent career woman, no time for men," she asserted, though my barb had clearly struck a nerve. With a dramatic huff, Shannon stormed off.

"Don't be mean, Junior," Mum gently chided, though she enjoyed our sibling banter.

Sweet Selena, always trying to ease tension, washed up Shannon's discarded dishes. My shy sister was unfailingly thoughtful, though she struggled with her own issues.

"How was your night with Dad?" Mum asked pointedly. I suspected lingering feelings remained, though he'd left her years ago.

"It was nice; we just talked sports at the pub," I summarised evasively.

"Tell me more! What'd you chat about?"

"Nothing too interesting honestly."

"Well, I love football - go Manchester Red Socks!" Mum asserted.

I stifled a chuckle at her obvious obliviousness. "Right, Red Socks, of course."

My sisters avoided the topic of Dad altogether. I understood their lingering hurt but wished we weren't so divided. What Dad did was wrong, but he was still family.

For all our issues, I hoped we could heal in time. We all had flaws, but we only had each other.

After breakfast, I retreated to my room to play video games before meeting up with friends. But first, I decided to check in on Shannon. I found her in her room blasting angry punk rock.

"Hey," I said, poking my head in.

"Sorry if I went too far at breakfast. Just some brotherly joking around, you know?"

"Ugh, it's fine," Shannon sighed, turning her music down.

"I just hate feeling like the loser sibling, the ageing spinster. But maybe I do need to get out more, meet people."

"There's no rush, you're only thirty," I said.

"But when the right guy comes along, you'll know. Just gotta be patient."

Shannon smiled reluctantly. "When did you get so wise, little bro?"

I grinned. "Hey, even I have my moments."

After making amends, I headed to Selena's room, finding her curled up reading as always.

"Hey sis, whatcha reading?" I asked.

She flushed pink, shyly showing me the cover of a romance novel.

I smiled kindly. "You'll find your Prince Charming someday too. Don't stress about it."

Selena nodded, flashing me a grateful smile. She didn't need to say anything - I understood.

Before meeting my friends, I found Mum watering her garden flowers, her safe haven.

"Gorgeous blooms," I complimented.

"Aren't they?" she beamed proudly.

"Nothing makes me happier than nurturing these beautiful plants. Like raising your kids - you'll always be my greatest joy."

I hugged her, overcome with love. For all the chaos our family endured, our bonds would outlast it all.

Today our family attempted a rare group outing - shopping at our local mall. Selena eagerly suggested catching a movie together, but the rest of us preferred an activity that allowed conversation. As the lone boy among chattering sisters, I'd come to not just tolerate but actually enjoy gossip.

I didn't need anything personally, but time together was the real treat. Shannon viewed it as an excuse to buy out stores if Mum would only fund her splurging, which she never did. But if sweet Selena asked, Mum tended to cave - clearly the favorite child. Not that I minded such dynamics.

"I just need new pyjamas," Selena offered by way of compromise.

So off we went to the tired mall in our sleepy hometown of Emberglade. Mum refused to shop anywhere beyond the city limits.

"We were born and raised here," she'd declare whenever I suggested branching out.

"No need to go elsewhere!" Our town was dismal, but Mum loved it stubbornly.

When I asked where to start, Shannon suggested Zara or Primark. Selena's eyes lit up at the mention of Zara.

"I absolutely love Zara!" The two often wore identical outfits - no surprise they loved the same stores.

I warned against lingering too long in Zara, but I doubted they'd listen. Soon Shannon emerged modelling hideous zebra print trousers.

"Think you can pull those off?" I smirked.

"Better than just wearing shorts every day," she shot back.

"Hey, the ladies love them," I retorted with a grin.

While Shannon shopped, Selena agonised over pyjamas with Mum's input. If I were here with Dad, we'd likely be playing tennis or watching football instead of clothes shopping. But time with my female family had its own charm.

After what felt like hours, Mum finally selected some pyjamas for indecisive Selena.

"You're twenty-eight, stop letting Mum dress you," I teased. Both shot me irritated looks.

"Enough bickering, you're acting like children," Mum scolded. She was right - together we often regressed into childish spats. But that's family. For better or worse, these were my people.

Selena retrieved her pyjamas, carefully selected by our mother.

"Do you really need Mum to choose your pyjamas?" I playfully teased, earning disapproving glances from both Selena and our mother.

"You can't talk, dear. Mum still handles your dishes and decides your meals," Selena retorted, her sharp comeback catching me off guard. It was a new side of her.

"That's enough, you two," Mum stepped in, her tone firm. She despised public confrontations, and in this instance, she was right.

Emerging from the shop, we strolled past a pub adorned with a sizeable TV broadcasting the latest news.

"Hold on, that can't be him," Shannon remarked, her initial intent seemingly to crack a joke.

"That's our father!"

Her words hit me like a sledgehammer. At first, I dismissed her with a scoff, but as I peered through the condensation-smeared glass window at the screen, my heart plummeted.

The headline read:

"Ten am: Layla Smith Found Dead in Suspect's Flat: James Jones at Emberglade."

Dread consumed me as they used a photograph of my father and Layla together as the headline image.

I turned to my mother, whose face had drained of colour, as if she were on the verge of fainting. Selena rushed over to provide comfort, leaving me standing there in disbelief. It was astonishing that Shannon, the last to react, had been the one to spot this unsettling news. She had never had the best relationship with our father, and her disdain for Layla was palpable, but I had expected a different response from her upon encountering such shocking headlines.

As my mother's tears streamed down her face, the bar's patrons gawked at our family's emotional turmoil. The suffocating gaze of strangers pressed upon us, compelling us to escape this intrusive scrutiny. We aided our distraught mother into the car, waiting for her to regain composure. It was Selena who took the wheel, as Mum was in no condition to drive.

Shock still gripped me tightly. How could my father, the man I thought I knew, be implicated in such a heinous act? I staunchly clung to the belief that he must have been framed. There could be no other explanation.

My mind was a tempest, a whirlwind of thoughts racing at breakneck speed. But I also couldn't ignore the agony that gripped my mother, the woman who had believed in my father's innocence.

Her world was unravelling before her eyes, and I struggled to comprehend the magnitude of her pain. What lay ahead for him? Had he concealed a monstrous side for years? Layla, always kind to me, had met a horrific end, and my heart ached for her.

Our sombre journey home was punctuated by my mother's unceasing sobs. I clung to my phone, desperately scouring the news for any evidence to refute the TV report, praying that it was a terrible mistake. Yet, my search yielded nothing but the grim headlines, solidifying the horrifying reality.

As we stepped into our house, Shannon flicked on the television, and the same ominous headline confronted us once more.

"Is this our life now? That... that man ruined our life!" Shannon's voice quivered with anger as her fist clenched. Her words stung, painting our father as a heartless cheater and now, potentially, a murderer.

I recoiled from her accusations, unwilling to accept them.

"No, Shan, stop it! This can't be true."

"Open your eyes, Junior. Does this look like a joke? Something that's not true?" Shannon retorted, her eyes filled with frustration.

"Our father is not capable of murder. I was with him last week." I was adamant he didn't do it.

"He's not the same man he was a few years ago. I don't know who this man is anymore. This is going to be with us for the rest of our lives," Shannon lamented.

Her words struck me like a bolt of lightning. We lived in a tight-knit small town, where everyone knew everyone else. We were now linked to a gruesome crime, and the judgmental eyes of our community would be inescapable. I was overcome with disbelief.

Our careers, our very lives, teetered on the precipice of irreparable change. Shannon, an aspiring actor, faced the threat of her professional prospects crumbling as her association with the accused murderer became public knowledge. Even my already-unpleasant job at the cafe seemed poised to become an unbearable ordeal, as our family's sudden notoriety threatened to eclipse everything we had known.

My mother gradually found her composure and began to accept the grim reality. Unsure if she was prepared to discuss it, I felt compelled to reach out to someone for reassurance.

"Mum, we'll be alright, won't we? Our jobs, our lives – will they remain unchanged?" Silence greeted my question.

I recalled the task of taking out the trash but hesitated to step outside, fearing the judgement of our community. I agonised over whether there had been any warning signs, praying that the tragedy hadn't occurred on a night we spent together. How could our father have inflicted this upon us and upon Layla? My mind was a whirlwind of questions and confusion, mirroring the turmoil that must have engulfed my mother.

Simultaneously, I harboured concerns for my father's uncertain fate. Had he concealed a dark side all along? Layla had always treated me with kindness and respect; she certainly didn't deserve such a tragic end.

CHAPTER 3

A stern voice broke through my swirling thoughts, demanding, "Open up, it's the police."

The timing couldn't have been worse; I had just learned about my father's alleged involvement, and now, they were here to interrogate me. My hands trembled, and my mouth went parched with anxiety.

My mother hurried to fetch a glass of water, and together, we approached the door. I couldn't predict their questions, but the fear of uttering the wrong words gnawed at me. I was determined not to incriminate myself when I had committed no wrongdoing.

We ushered the two police officers into our home, where my mother offered them tea, a gesture they both declined. One of them began,

"I'm not sure if you've heard, but it's related to your father. James, we have some questions for you. You were with him the other night, correct?" The urge to deny any connection to my father's recent actions clawed at me, but my commitment to truth prevailed. It had indeed been an innocent night out with my dad, and I had nothing to hide.

Reluctantly, I nodded and replied,

"Yes, I was with him." The interrogation had begun, and I could only hope that my cooperation would eventually unveil the truth behind the grim events that had unfolded.

"James, are you aware of the recent developments?" one of the officers inquired with a measured tone.

"Yes, sir," I replied, my voice tinged with unease,

"I've seen it on the news."

The gravity of the situation hung heavily in the room. The officer continued,

"Alright, then you understand the seriousness of this matter. Can you provide an account of what transpired on the night you were out with your father?"

"We just went to a pub, had a few drinks, and watched a football game, there wasn't much else to it." I explained.

"We've received reports that your father may have been behaving in an intimidating way toward others. Staring aggressively at them in the pub," he pressed.

"Were you in any way involved or encouraging this behaviour?"

"No, not at all," I asserted firmly.

"To the best of my knowledge, he didn't engage in any such conduct."

The officer's gaze remained unwavering.

"I must emphasise, James, your father is facing very serious charges. I need you to be completely forthright with me. Can you tell me what time you left the pub and in what condition your father was at that moment?"

"He was a bit intoxicated," I admitted,

"But it's not unusual for us to have a couple of drinks together; it's how we socialise. I left around ten pm."

"Did you leave alone?" the officer inquired further.

"Yes," I confirmed,

"I left on my own." My sense of trepidation grew as the questioning continued, recognising that my responses were critical in the unfolding investigation into my father's actions.

The tension in the room intensified as the police officers sifted through their stack of questions and evidence, heightening my unease. Every word uttered was carefully transcribed, and the weight of their scrutiny bore down on me.

The officers continued to ask me plenty of questions, I tried my best to give them the answers they needed, by telling the truth.

The interview with me concluded, and their attention shifted toward the rest of my family.

"Tessa, Shannon, and Selena, may we have a moment of your time?" one of the officers requested.

My mother's discomfort was palpable. Nervousness radiated from everyone except Shannon, who seemed oddly intrigued by the situation. I silently hoped she understood the gravity of the matter – this wasn't an act; our father could be involved in something unthinkable. The sickness in the pit of my stomach persisted.

The officers began their inquiries,

"Could you all describe your relationship with James Senior?"

A moment of hesitation hung in the air before Shannon, ever eager to speak her mind, answered first.

"Not really. He cheated on our mum, and I've never forgiven him."

Tears welled up in my mother's eyes as she struggled to speak through her runny nose and wet cheeks.

"Yes, he cheated on me, but the man I knew could not... could not commit murder."

Selena's response was more measured,

"I still love him; after all, he's my father. But I haven't seen him in years."

The officers asked a few more questions. Recognising that my mother was in no condition to continue, and Selena appeared shaken, the police concluded the interview, thanking us for our cooperation.

Although I harboured resentment at their questioning, I knew they were just doing their job, trying to unravel the truth behind the horrifying allegations.

Once they left, our home fell into an agonising silence. My mother crumpled to the floor, tears flowing unabated, and Selena joined her in a shared anguish. Shannon and I struggled to maintain a facade of strength, but our hearts ache in silence. I wouldn't wish this torment on anyone. We were a loving family, despite our imperfections, and Layla, a victim in all of this, deserved nothing but praise.

During the following week, I found solace in the seclusion of my room, reluctant to face the world beyond our home's walls. The only time I ventured downstairs was for our family meals, though dining together amidst the prevailing cloud of depression, stress, and overwhelming uncertainty made for sombre evenings. On this particular night, Mother had prepared chicken pasta, and we gathered at the table.

"Thank you, Mum, this is lovely," I offered, trying to lighten the atmosphere.

"How are you feeling today?" Her response was a forced smile and an evasive disregard of my question.

Shannon decided to divert our attention from the distressing reality.

"I'm thinking of changing my hair colour," she announced.

"No way, to what?" Selena responded with a hint of sarcasm, typical of our family's interactions.

It seemed impossible for us to have a straightforward conversation, but maybe discussing hair was better than dwelling on the ruin of our lives.

Shannon elaborated,

"I'm considering going brunette."

"You've been blonde your whole life; are you sure?" I asked.

"I'm sure. I'll look great," Shannon confidently replied.

"Yeah, I'm sure you will," I added with a sarcastic remark, sharing a knowing glance with Selena. A brief chuckle escaped Shannon, breaking the tension.

Meanwhile, Mother seemed lost in her thoughts, her gaze fixed on the ceiling, untouched food on her plate. Her appetite had waned, another casualty of the ongoing turmoil.

As we finished our meal and cleared the table, I retreated to my room, seeking refuge in the numbing glow of the television. In the distance, I could hear Shannon and Selena in another room, their quiet sobs a testament to the shared pain we all harboured. I longed to release my own emotions, but the overwhelming weight of it all had left me too drained even to shed a tear.

A phone call from the police left me with no choice but to head to the police station, a place I had never set foot in before and never wished to visit. Uncertain about the dress code, I settled on black joggers and the same blue top I had worn on that fateful night. Anxiety clenched my chest, making the idea of facing the public seem unbearable, so I opted for an Uber to get me there.

As I waited for the ride, my mind raced with apprehensions. What would they ask me? How could I provide answers that would help in such a grave situation?

Finally, the Uber arrived, and a few moments of small talk with the driver served as a brief distraction from the mounting tension. The journey to the police station felt interminable, the weight of the unknown bearing down on me.

Upon arrival, an officer directed me to a small, austere room, dominated by a long table in the centre. Nerves gripped me like a vice, prompting me to reach for a glass of water placed before me. The seconds seemed to stretch into minutes as I awaited the arrival of the officers who had come to my house previously.

The door opened, and in walked the two familiar officers, clutching their papers, which bore not only notes but also what appeared to be photographs. Their demeanour was stern, and Officer Bellis wasted no time, adopting an assertive tone.

"Do you know of anyone else who saw Layla that night?" he questioned.

I hesitated, trying to recall any potential witnesses.

"No, I don't think so."

Officer Bellis wasn't one to mince words.

"Think harder, kid! Time is of the essence here."

Struggling to conjure any additional memories, I stammered,

"I... I did, um, no, sir."

"Alright," Officer Bellis responded, his tone softening slightly.

"We're not trying to intimidate you. This is a very serious case, and we need accurate information."

"I understand, Officer" I replied, taking a deep breath, attempting to gather my composure amidst the relentless whirlwind of emotions.

Their initial attempt at intimidation had left me rattled, but as they sensed my growing fear, the officers decided to adopt a more approachable demeanour.

I recounted every detail I could remember: the clothing my father had worn, the timeframe of our outing from five pm to ten pm. When the police revealed that my father had departed just twelve minutes after my exit, a chilling unease settled over me.

I struggled to reconcile the image of the man I had seen that night with the notion of a potential murderer. What did a person planning such a heinous act look like? Despite the alcohol in my system, my memory remained remarkably clear, providing a vivid recollection of the evening's events.

"We're going to show you some images now," officer Humphries stated, his tone grave. Dread coiled in my stomach. Would they display gruesome crime scene photos? I braced myself.

Humphries continued,

"Here's a picture of your father leaving the pub. Pay close attention to his hands; he appears to be putting on these black gloves. Have you ever seen him wear these gloves before?"

I scrutinised the image, a shiver crawling down my spine. Those gloves were unfamiliar to me.

"No, I haven't seen him wear these before."

Relief washed over me as they assured me they had obtained the information they needed. With their questioning concluded, they offered to drive me home, a gesture I welcomed wholeheartedly. My ordeal in the police station was over, at least for now.

As I left, gratitude welled up within me that they had summoned me for questioning instead of someone else in my family. The weight of this investigation would likely break them instantly. Shannon, in her own way, might attempt to deflect the anguish with humour and feigned nonchalance. I knew, however, that beneath her facade, she too carried the burden of grief.

I prayed fervently that this sinister chapter in our lives would come to a close, that we could somehow move forward and regain the sense of security that had been shattered.

CHAPTER 4

Two months had crawled by since the chilling revelation that my father had committed a gruesome murder, and the torment had become a relentless shadow, haunting every facet of our lives. Our family had been thrust into a nightmarish existence, enduring unimaginable trials that no one should ever have to face.

My mother, a dedicated high school teacher, had clung to her work as a lifeline amid the storm. But the relentless barrage of hatred from a merciless public had pierced her heart like a thousand daggers. The whispers of onlookers painted her as an accomplice, blaming her for not preventing the monstrous act.

They failed to see the stark difference between the man she had married thirty-two years ago and the monster he had become.

Even the innocence of children had been tainted by this pervasive darkness. The taunts they hurled at my mother were nothing short of cruel.

"She shagged a murderer," they would jeer.

"I bet she was happy he killed her," they would insinuate, their words dripping with venom.

The sheer audacity of such comments left me seething with anger and disbelief. What has become of compassion and empathy in the hearts of the young?

The parents, regrettably, were no better. Their judgmental stares and thinly veiled contempt painted a bleak portrait of humanity. My sisters, Selena and Shannon, bore their own burdens of scorn and judgement. Selena, working as a cleaner, found herself isolated from people but confronted negativity whenever she dared to venture out.

Shannon, once a blossoming actor, had seen her career plummet into an abyss of rejection. The opportunities that once beckoned now lay in ruins, replaced by a relentless deluge of 'James Senior, the deranged killer' splashed across every television screen.

A brand that had once embraced her had now severed all ties, leaving her to navigate a bleak and uncertain future.

As for me, I had taken a hiatus from work, but the impending return loomed like a gathering storm. Nervousness coiled within me like a venomous serpent, each step toward my workplace laden with trepidation. I faced the daunting prospect of enduring the public's scrutiny and derision, a trial by fire that awaited me as I embarked on my daily journey via public transport.

I stood at the bus stop, my car had no petrol, which made the journey much worse, a tense knot of anxiety coiling within me, my heart pounding like a relentless drum. Fifteen minutes had passed, and during that time, I had endured the harsh cacophony of honking horns and the cruel jeers of passersby, their words a jagged assault on my already fragile psyche. I couldn't discern the specific insults hurled my way, but I knew they were anything but kind.

Finally, the number forty-four bus, the solitary lifeline to my workplace, appeared on the horizon. I raised my arm to signal its approach, the familiar trepidation of boarding public transport washing over me. As I stepped onto the bus, I was met with an instant barrage of piercing stares that seemed to bore into my very soul. It was as if the passengers shared a collective desire to see me punished, their gazes delivering a relentless onslaught.

Desperate to shield myself from their judgement, I took a seat at the front, away from prying eyes. The eight-minute journey ahead felt like an eternity as the weight of their judgement bore down upon me.

The bus came to a halt to accommodate a new passenger, a tall and imposing figure, his shoulders carved from solid stone. He, too, was headed to my destination. Retrieving his ticket, our eyes locked in a moment of unsettling connection. My gaze instinctively darted away, but his unwavering stare persisted, drawing him closer to me.

"May I sit here?" he inquired, his voice a mere whisper, his demeanour oddly calm.

"Of course," I responded, unable to muster a refusal, though my instincts screamed otherwise.

I settled into my seat, a stifling sense of awkwardness enveloping me as his gaze continued to linger upon me. It felt as if he bore a secret, as if he knew who I was.

"I understand what you're going through," he confided in a hushed tone, leaning closer until his words brushed against my ear.

I recoiled, stunned by the audacity of his statement. How could he possibly comprehend the torment that had engulfed my life? It wasn't the kind of experience one could easily relate to, especially not in a town as small and tight-knit as ours, even if it did have its rough edges.

"I'm a therapist," he continued, his words an unexpected revelation.

"I work with clients who have endured the darkest of trials, much like yourself."

His unsolicited confession left me baffled. Why had this stranger chosen to sit beside me and disclose his profession? Did he view me as broken and in need of help? Maybe I was, but I had been determined to maintain an appearance of strength, to pretend that the turmoil surrounding me hadn't inflicted lasting wounds. Yet, deep down, I knew the truth – I was profoundly wounded, and the scars run deeper than anyone could see.

"If you ever need me, here's my card," he offered, extending a small, inconspicuous piece of paper bearing the words

The card read 'Oliver, Licensed therapist'. The card featured contact details for his website and a phone number belonging to him. It may sound peculiar, but in that moment, as the card exchanged hands, a profound sense of relief washed over me. It felt as though, for the first time, I had someone I could turn to, someone who might help me navigate the turbulent waters of my life.

Oliver exuded a calming presence, his demeanour carrying a reassuring weight that enveloped me. It was a peculiar comfort, but it made me feel safe, as though the daunting prospect of therapy might offer a chance at healing and a fresh start.

The bus jolted to a halt as Oliver pressed the bell to signal our stop, the place where both of us would disembark.

"Take care, Junior," he bid me farewell, and for a brief moment, the use of the term 'Junior' by someone outside of my family felt oddly unfamiliar.

Stepping off the bus, I found myself standing before the familiar sight of my café, just across the road. A measure of tension had dissipated during the uneventful bus ride, with nothing more taxing than a few disdainful glances. My former coworkers still occupied their positions, their presence a reassuring anchor amidst the turmoil that had gripped my life.

However, lurking in the shadows of my apprehension was the ever-present dread of encountering Layla's father. He had been a regular customer, visiting every Monday and Friday for his coffee fix. Today marked another Monday, raising the spectre of an encounter. Yet, I couldn't help but think that he, too, had likely altered his routine in the wake of the tragic events.

As I entered Glaze Cafe, the quiet ambience greeted me with a sense of relief. Only two patrons were savouring their meals, a welcome sight that promised fewer prying eyes and less stress. With determined resolve, I strode through the room, seeking refuge in the bustling kitchen.

"James is back!" The enthusiastic chorus from the café's staff filled the air as they rushed forward, enveloping me in warm hugs and heartfelt greetings.

Their genuine expressions of having missed me touched me deeply. I had fretted endlessly about how I would be perceived, only to realise that my judgement had been unfairly directed toward them. They treated me as if nothing had ever happened, a return to the normalcy I had so desperately craved.

As the café began to fill with more patrons, most of the staff completed their shifts, leaving me alone with my manager. I expertly brewed coffees and served them to eager customers, while my manager deftly handled the orders. It felt like a return to the comforting routine I had missed.

However, a sudden shout disrupted the newfound tranquility.

"Oi!" The voice crackled with anger, instantly setting my heart racing. Could it be Layla's father?

A man rose from his seat, leaving behind an unfinished meal, fork still clenched tightly in hand. Yet, I couldn't place his face; this was not Layla's father.

Curiosity mingled with fear as I wondered who this stranger was and what he might say to me.

"I work here, sir. Is everything okay?" I attempted to maintain politeness, but my words only seemed to stoke his ire.

"Your dad killed my best friend!" His voice quivered with grief and rage.

"I could kill you. If you come near here again, I'll wrap my hands around your throat, you women-beating murderer."

My tongue felt tied, the words of apology or explanation remaining trapped within me. It wasn't Layla's father but her best friend, a man consumed by anguish over the loss of someone dear to him. I stood there, unable to find the words, bearing witness to his anguish as he vented his pain and frustration.

"Come on now, Luton, let him be," a voice from the crowd implored, likely his mother, attempting to defuse the volatile situation.

It was my first encounter with this man named Luton, his face contorted with grief, his dark, bushy eyebrows furrowed, and his voice a desperate cry for justice. His agony mirrored my own in the months that had passed, a stark reminder that forgiveness might forever remain out of reach, casting doubt on my continued employment at the café.

Relieved of my duties early by my manager, I made my way back home, grateful to have avoided Layla's father but haunted by the image of her best friend's anguished face, the embodiment of pain and loss.

Arriving home marked the end of a terrible day at work. The calendar displayed November twenty-third, five pm, a date we had collectively chosen to re-enter the workforce. Our financial situation had become dire, classifying us as a struggling family. Our humble abode, a testament to our modest means, was a stark reminder of our parents' perpetual financial struggles.

I opted for the back entrance, sidestepping the clutter of old clothes and boxes that still lay abandoned near the front door. No one had the energy to address the mess; our minds were consumed by the relentless turmoil that had engulfed our lives.

As I ventured into the living room, I found Shannon there, wearing an unusually radiant smile. I couldn't help but ask,

"Hey Shan, are you okay?"

Shannon responded with a huge smile and a quick nod.

Her response left me puzzled. Why was she so elated? Such genuine smiles had been scarce in our household for months.

Perplexed, I pressed further,

"What's got you in such high spirits?" She leaned in, her eyes gleaming with an air of excitement, and shared her revelation,

"Have you not seen, Junior? Father has pleaded not guilty."

The news struck me like a bolt from the blue.

"Are you serious?" I queried, my disbelief apparent.

Shannon reassured me, her words laden with a strange mix of hope and uncertainty.

"No, look, I promise. What if he didn't do it?"

I was left grappling with conflicting emotions. My initial conviction, that my father could never commit murder, had given way to a harsher reality. But if he had indeed pleaded not guilty, what did that imply? Was there a possibility of his innocence?

The conversation with Shannon left me bewildered, torn between two divergent narratives.

Summoning my courage, I posed a direct question to my sister, seeking her unfiltered opinion.

"Shannon, I need you to be honest with me. Do you think Dad killed her?" I was hoping for a positive answer from her.

"If I'm being honest, yes. I hope he rots in prison."

Her words struck like a dagger to my heart. Shannon's revelation was chilling, her conviction unwavering. She held no sympathy for either our father or Layla, the victim. It was a stark departure from her previous teasing demeanour. I couldn't fathom the depths of this newfound cruelty. Why would she find solace in death? Perhaps the smile she shared was evil.

Before I could further probe her unsettling revelation, the return of our mother and Selena diverted the conversation. They had just returned from a trip to the cinema, to distract themselves from the grim reality that had become our lives. Distraction had become our refuge, a means to navigate the turbulent waters of our father's uncertain fate.

"Finally went to the cinema then, Selena?" I inquired, noticing the fatigue in her eyes.

"Yeah, it was amazing. We watched a thriller movie about there being no rules in the world," she responded, her enthusiasm tempered by the grim reality that surrounded us.

The choice of film, with its anarchic premise, seemed incongruous given our current circumstances.

"Mum loved it too, didn't you, Mum?" Selena chimed in, prompting our mother's reluctant agreement. Yet, her demeanour betrayed her true feelings; it was evident that the film hadn't brought her the enjoyment she pretended to derive from it.

My mother had always been a selfless woman, going to great lengths to ensure our happiness, even in our adulthood. It was why she accompanied Selena to the cinema, extending her role as a loving mother to that of a supportive friend.

Shannon, my older sister, then rose from her seat as if preparing to make an announcement. I had a hunch she was about to broach the subject of our father's recent plea of not guilty.

"Can we all agree on something, guys?" Shannon began, and the room fell silent as we paused the TV, eager to hear her proposition.

"No more mourning or taking slander from strangers," she declared with unwavering resolve.

"We agreed that this was the date we'd all move on. That man is dead to us. We shall not speak of his name again."

CHAPTER 5

Later that evening, as James and his family grappled with the challenge of moving forward without their father, a parallel drama unfolded at the opposite end of Emberglade. The enigmatic figure known as The Onyx prowled the streets, shrouded in a cloak of all-black and grey attire, resembling an oversized spectre.

These late-night excursions through Emberglade were far from commonplace, earning the town its eerie moniker as a "ghost town" after dark. The mysterious wanderer advanced at an unhurried pace, head perpetually bowed, seemingly guided by an unerring sense of direction.

Veering right, they entered a narrower lane flanked by four imposing houses. The attention of The Onyx, concealed beneath the hood's shadowy veil, was drawn to one particular house. It was a daunting task to discern any facial features beneath the obscure attire. This chosen house stood in stark contrast to its neighbours, enveloped in darkness, save for the solitary bedroom light on the first floor.

Intruding without invitation, The Onyx pushed the door ajar, ensuring its silent closure. They scoured the downstairs, methodically checking each nook and cranny for any unwanted guests. Satisfied with the preliminary sweep, they began their ascent up the creaking staircase. Each step emitted a discordant protest, making it nearly impossible for their presence to remain undetected.

"Hello?!" Panic infused the homeowner's voice as the unsettling realisation dawned that an uninvited visitor may be lurking within their home, and they were utterly alone.

"Is anyone there?" Torn between the impulse to confront the intruder and escaping through the closed window, they weighed their options. Though the prospect of leaping from the first-floor window was daunting, it appeared a preferable alternative to facing a potential home invader head-on.

Darkness enveloped the room as they flicked off the lights, hoping to evade Onyx's notice. But Onyx already knew exactly where they were hiding. In one swift motion, Onyx threw open the door and spotted a figure trying to slide out the window. As the homeowner desperately scrambled through, Onyx raced over, knife glinting. Just as they were about to drop outside, Onyx's blade found its mark, piercing their spine. A twisted smile crossed Onyx's face as the knife was yanked free, sending the homeowner tumbling headfirst out the window in a trail of blood.

Onyx left no traces on the body except for the bloodstained knife. Donning plastic covers and thick gloves, Onyx quickly slipped into the night.

The next morning, the news reached the Jones family.

"Junior, did you hear?" Selena asked, visibly distraught.

Junior clung to a shred of hope it wasn't more tragedy.

"What is it?"

"It's Dad...and Aunt Janice too." Selena choked up.

"She was murdered last night." Tears pouring down her face.

James reeled in dismay. Their father arrested, now Aunt Janice dead? He felt the walls closing in, fears rising that he or his family could be next.

As Shannon and Mum joined them, solemn and shaken, a heavy silence settled. No one wanted to discuss the horrors further. Junior felt isolated, needing to talk without judgement.

Suddenly he remembered the therapist from the bus, Oliver. Retrieving his card, James texted urgently:

"Hi Oliver, it's James. Great meeting you. I desperately need a session as soon as possible. Please let me know."

Minutes later came the reply:

"You're booked for tomorrow morning, Junior. See you then."

Being called "Junior" brought back memories of their encounter. He looked forward to the therapy session, finally having someone to listen to.

The next morning, James arrived early at Oliver's office, taken aback by its grandeur—how could one therapist need this whole building? Perhaps he lived here too. James texted Oliver that he was outside rather than ringing the intimidating bell. Oliver remotely unlocked the door in response.

Inside, signs directed visitors to the third-floor therapy suite. Opting for the stairs over the elevator, Junior climbed up anxiously. Confined spaces like elevators unnerved him, especially with his fear of breaking down trapped inside. Although after the recent murders, even that seemed trivial.

"Welcome, Junior, have a seat," Oliver greeted him.

"Thanks for seeing me last minute," Junior sighed, sitting down.

"I'm so overwhelmed lately."

"Understandably so after everything that's happened. How are you coping with all this stress?" Oliver asked gently.

Junior hesitated before opening up.

"My dad's case is all over the news, and now he's pleading innocent. I'd finally accepted he could be guilty. And now my aunt was just murdered. I...." Junior broke down struggled to finish his sentence. Confused and hurt, not wanting to accept this is now his life. He bravely continues.

"I'm scared for my family's safety."

Oliver nodded sympathetically.

"That's an incredible burden. Your feelings are completely valid. How is this impacting you emotionally?"

"I'm trying to stay strong, but it's hard. Seeing my family so depressed when we used to be happy and carefree. I don't know who to trust anymore."

"You clearly have immense love for your family. But remember to prioritise your own wellbeing too." Oliver remained professional and followed his list of responses.

"I know, that's why I reached out to you. This is my first step."

"I'm glad you did, and I'll support you fully," Oliver affirmed.

"Anything shared here is strictly confidential. So please, speak your mind."

Junior felt the floodgates open, grateful to finally unburden himself. With Oliver bearing compassionate witness, he began to process the turmoil churning within.

The therapy session with Oliver had been cathartic for Junior. Finally opening up and voicing his struggles lifted a weight from his shoulders. At home, he hid his pain to seem strong as the only male. But Oliver's kindness and empathy created a safe space for Junior to process everything. He decided regular therapy would be beneficial and drove him. With his car finally fixed.

As they drove, Junior noticed a crowd up ahead. Squinting, he could make out their angry signs reading

"Jones Family are Murderers!" James' heart sank.

The whole town had turned against them, blaming his family for the killings. In an instant, the positivity from therapy evaporated. Would life ever feel normal again?

Among the mob, Junior recognised two faces - Luton, the man who had confronted him at work, and Alfie, his dad's best friend.

He had seen Alfie at the pub with his dad that fateful final night. Why was he now amongst this hateful crowd? Junior knew his dad's relationship with Layla had flaws, though he always painted it idyllically. Did Alfie resent Layla for coming between them?

Junior racked his brain, unable to recall his dad ever interacting with Layla's family. Alfie barely knew Junior outside of the pub. Still, seeing his dad's friend aligned against them crushed Junior. He longed for his old happy life, now seemingly out of reach forever.

But Junior couldn't just focus on his family's safety - he felt compelled to uncover this killer's identity himself, before anyone else got hurt. If the authorities wouldn't help, he would do whatever necessary to protect his loved ones.

CHAPTER 6

Get them out, get them out!"
The enraged mob's chants echoed through the once-peaceful streets, their fervour unmistakable.

On this ominous night, the dark cloud of hostility had converged yet again, and this time, it loomed menacingly in front of the Jones family's very home.

At the forefront of this hostile congregation were two familiar faces that James Junior had observed during his taxi ride: Luton and Alfie.

It was Alfie who initiated the fiery chants with his commanding Geordie accent and a set of lungs that could rattle the heavens. His voice pierced the night air, rallying the crowd against the Jones family, while Luton stood firmly by his side.

As the mob relentlessly cried out, Alfie tapped Luton on the shoulder, signalling a need for a private conversation amidst the tumultuous sea of voices.

With a nod, they stepped aside, leaving the remaining forty individuals to continue their vehement chants. In the shadow of the night, their intentions remained ominous.

"This guy's in for it, Luton," Alfie declared, his voice edged with determination.

Luton, wearing a wide grin that hinted at deeper malevolence, responded,

"You know I've been waiting for this day, Alfie. How could you ever have been best mates with a bloke like him?" Luton asked.

Alfie cast a disdainful glance toward the Jones family's residence, confessed,

"I never liked that guy. Always moping around, even though he had a beautiful girlfriend." It was then that Luton's face registered genuine surprise.

"She was a beauty," Luton admitted.

"Can I share something with you, Alfie? I think I was in love with her, and he snatched her away from me." The revelation hung heavily in the air, an unexpected confession that caught both men off guard.

However, Alfie had one more revelation to unveil.

"I don't blame you," he admitted, his voice fraught with the weight of unspoken truths.

"I know we've been mates for years, but you've got to know this: Layla and I were together a month before she passed. I was falling for her too."

In that moment, the camaraderie between Luton and Alfie shifted, revealing deep-seated wounds and buried desires. Despite their years of friendship, this newfound revelation had the power to reshape the dynamics between them, as it unveiled a complex web of emotions and tangled loyalties that could no longer be ignored.

Tensions escalated rapidly, Luton let the emotions get the better of him and got aggressive.

"You knew I loved her. Yes, we were only friends, but so were you. You could have been the reason he killed her!" Luton made a wild claim in his outburst of rage after hearing Alfie's secret.

Alfie wasn't one to play games.

"Speak to me like that again, I'll knock you out in front of this crowd, you muppet," he spat, jabbing his finger in Luton's face.

Luton slapped his hand away angrily. In one swift motion, Alfie head butted Luton's nose, blood instantly gushing. Though Luton stumbled back, he remained on his feet. Alfie followed up with a crushing punch to his jaw, sending Luton crashing to the concrete.

As the mob pulled them apart, Alfie shouted after him,

"Learned your lesson now, yeah?"

Two scorned men, both obsessed with a woman who'd never been theirs. Now with Layla tragically gone, they channelled their pain into hatred for James Senior.

Alfie grabbed a taxi, leaving Luton's goons to tend to him. They held no alliance.

"The town's rumours would spread every day about the murders in Emberglade. Could either Alfie or Luton have been behind the murder of James Senior's sister?"

At home, Alfie's brain-damaged brother Joel waited helplessly. During a childhood accident, severe head trauma had left Thirty-year-old Joel immobile and voiceless, requiring Alfie's constant care.

Cleaning himself up, Alfie regretted losing control with Luton.

He needed to remain focused for Joel's sake. Other than his part time carer, his poor brother depended on him totally.

"Hey little guy," Alfie whispered, caressing Joel's cheek. Joel blinked slowly in response, his version of affection.

As Alfie gazed into Joel's vacant eyes, he hardened his resolve. He would find justice for Layla, no matter what it took. He owed that to the memory of the woman they both loved.

Caring for Joel ended Alfie's boxing dreams, fuelling his bitterness at life's injustice. Despite frequent fights and police trouble, he couldn't abandon Joel, determined to protect him as he wished he'd protected Layla.

After Alfie's beating, Luton's crew drove him home, face bloodied and swollen. Luton agonised whether the public thrashing or knowing Alfie slept with Layla hurt more.

For years Luton desperately loved Layla, willing to do anything for her. Unable to get out the friend-zone. Now, returning alone to his cluttered flat, her absence ached painfully. Declining a hospital visit, he preferred nursing his wounds in isolation.

Except for Layla, Luton always rejected help. She cooked, provided company, and gave advice. Now takeout containers and whiskey bottles littered his home, reflecting his unmanaged grief.

Luton, consumed by the desire to make James Senior suffer as he had, knew that even that couldn't heal his pain. All he had left was hate.

This was a new side of Luton that others hadn't seen – an angry, hurt man who was once a happy, outgoing person but no longer. He made a plea to himself that he would do whatever it takes to get Layla the justice she deserves.

Amongst the vengeful mob, Terry nurtured his own simmering grudge. He worked with James Junior, serving Layla and James Senior when they dined out. Unlike their polite son, they rudely ridiculed Terry's looks and walk.

Terry was a man who would keep his cards close to his chest. No one truly knew the man he was. He still lives with his mother and his step dad. Who he hates.

Terry believed his stepdad and James Senior shared similar qualities, a deep resentment for his stepdad fuelled by hatred, yet he refrained from causing physical harm due to his love for his mother. To fill the emotional void, Terry sought alternative means.

One fateful day, Terry covertly inserted a glass shard into James Senior's food, resulting in weeks of internal bleeding. Terry derived satisfaction from his anonymous revenge, yearning for James Senior to discover the truth behind this malevolent act. Given his profound resentment, Terry might be capable of further vindictive actions.

Furthermore, the identity of "The Onyx" remains a mystery, as it could be anyone connected with James Senior.

CHAPTER 7

Today is therapy day, but before I head out, I want to touch base with my family about how they're coping and discuss my own feelings with Oliver.

"Food's ready, lovelies," Mum calls us down for the sausage toasties she's prepared.

Sausage toasties are Shannon's favourite; she adores how Mum cooks them.

"Nice bedhead, Selena." Shannon jokingly says

"Thanks, it's my signature style."

"If that's your style, then sure."

I steer clear of getting involved in these sorts of sisterly banter sessions. Whenever I join in on their girl talk, they tend to gang up on me.

Playful teasing is how our family expresses affection, but my mother's love shines through in the way she takes care of us. Despite my sisters being twenty eight and Thirty years old, she still prepares breakfast for them every morning.

"You look beautiful this morning, Mum," Selena's sweetness rubs Shannon the wrong way because she's quite the opposite.

"Ah, thank you, lovely. That's how I managed to raise three beautiful children," my mother says this, but she knows I resemble my dad.

She convinces herself that I look like her because that's what she wants to believe.

It's not pleasant being labelled as the child of a murderer, especially sharing his name and looking like him. but I guess that's the harsh reality, or is it? My dad pleaded not guilty, and I can't fathom why he would do that if he were the one who committed the crime.

I yearn to see him, peer into his eyes, and ask him whether he did it and why. Part of me clings to the hope that he's innocent, but maybe that's just a delusion fuelled by my desperate desire for things to return to normal.

With Mother and Selena leaving the room, it's the perfect opportunity to confide in Shannon about my inner turmoil.

I whisper to her, "Shannon, he pleaded not guilty, and his trial is next week. Maybe he's not a murderer!"

"Maybe, Junior, but I doubt it. Let's not forget there's someone else out there committing murder because of him. The outcome doesn't really matter." She coldly replies.

I knew she was right. This other murderer, nicknamed "Onyx" by the news, must be connected to my dad, given that they killed my auntie.

It can't be a mere coincidence. I have no idea who despises my father this much, or perhaps it's the love they had for Layla that's driven them to this.

Either way, I'm determined to find out. I'm tired of waiting and wondering; I'd rather take action myself. I realise it might be dangerous, but I have nothing to lose. My family's lives are at stake, and I'm willing to do whatever it takes.

I arrived at Oliver's office, and he buzzed me into his therapy room. I thought there might be less to discuss this time, but things just keep getting worse.

"Welcome back, Junior. It's great to see you again. How have you been holding up?"

I sighed, "I'm not sure. I feel like I'm bottling everything up mentally. It's really draining, but I don't want to come across as sad all the time. I'd rather keep it all in my head. But here I am, letting it all out to you."

Oliver nodded. "That's a positive step, Junior. You're taking care of yourself. I heard your father pleaded not guilty. What are your thoughts on that?"

I raised an eyebrow, "Been keeping up with the news, have you? Yes, the trial is next week. I'm thinking of attending. I want to witness him saying he didn't do it with my own eyes. I want to believe it, but I'm not sure I can. My opinion changes every day."

Oliver smiled. "Your father probably did it, James. He's not a nice man. You might not believe it, but you're coping quite well. I think you're doing a great job."

I was puzzled by Oliver's unprofessional comment about my father, as if he knew him personally. Maybe he was just following the news and making assumptions. But nobody truly knows him. I wasn't even sure I knew what kind of man he was.

"Has anything else happened in your life recently?"

I knew he was already aware of what's going on. I reply but confused by his new approach.

"Yeah, my auntie..." I couldn't finish the sentence; the emotions were catching up with me. I started crying in front of a man I'd only met a few times.

I wiped away my tears. "My aunt was murdered."

"I'm so sorry," Oliver said gently.

"How does that make you feel?"

I snapped angrily, "What do you think?!"

Oliver chuckled softly. "Let's take a breath, Junior. I'm here to help."

I sighed. "Sorry, I don't know where that came from."

"It's understandable with everything you're dealing with. I think we should end today's session here. You did a great job opening up."

He ended the session very early knowing the conversation was going to turn sour.

I was stunned by my outburst - I never raised my voice. Usually, I internalise stress, but therapy was releasing a torrent of emotions. I knew Oliver understood.

Now I needed to figure out my plan to find the killer, who could strike again anytime. Our town was small, and I'd recognise most faces. That thought terrified me - they may know me too.

I go into town to meet a friend for dinner. Entering the busy restaurant, I ignore the stares and whispers. My family plan on moving on with life, and so will I.

The staff seats me at a table. As I browse the menu, the room turns to gawk as if I've invaded their space. I send my tardy friend a text and wait.

Suddenly, a large man walked up behind me. His huge hand struck the side of my head, nearly knocking me down. I jumped up, ready to fight, as the man's wife splashed her wine on me. I thought, 'Of course, I wore white tonight.' But I also thought that this man wanted to kill me, and I'd have to fight for my life.

Before I can react, a staff member approaches. Thankfully she'll eject them so I can just enjoy my meal in a stained shirt.

But she walks past the couple and stands before me.

"I'm going to have to ask you to leave," she says firmly.

"We don't serve your kind here."

I reel in shock. "Me? I was assaulted!"

But of course - they see me as guilty, as James Senior. Not Junior. I am my own man. Why can't they see this?

Fighting back angry tears, I keep my head high. The injustice stings deeply. But I refuse to stoop to their level.

"You need to leave now, sir," the staff member states firmly.

I'm stunned. "Did you see what they just did to me?"

"I don't care, you need to go," she repeats coldly.

I look around desperately, hoping someone will take my side. But no one does.

Shannon was wrong, that we could go back to normal life. This proves that's impossible. I'm lucky the couple wasn't armed. They came out of nowhere while I sat reading the menu. This is a harsh wake-up call about being in public now.

I have to cancel with my sympathetic friend, who even lodges a complaint. But I tell him not to bother - it won't change how people see me.

The fear in their eyes says it all.

My father may be the killer, or maybe not. We'll find out at his trial. But either way, the real murderer is still loose, leaving us all potential targets.

In time, I hope the truth will emerge. But for now, I must accept this hostile reality and proceed carefully. It's senseless to fight against blind hatred. I will remain strong, keep my loved ones close, and do what's needed to survive each day.

With compassion and wisdom, we will endure this darkness together. I cannot control how others judge me, only how I react. And I refuse to let cruelty harden my heart. This too shall pass.

CHAPTER 8

With one kill already accomplished, The Onyx was relentless, moving swiftly to their next target. Their identity remained shrouded in mystery, a phantom haunting the town of Emberglade. Unbeknownst to anyone, they harboured sinister plans, intent on sowing chaos and fear.

Once again, the Onyx ventured into the nocturnal streets, cloaked in dark attire. This time, they concealed their face with a mask, determined to elude any prying cameras that might unveil their true identity. Standing vigil outside a corner shop, a weathered and forlorn establishment struggling to keep its doors open until the late hours, The Onyx watched the clock. It was ten-thirty PM, and closing time loomed. A woman approached, passing by the Onyx to enter the shop.

This encounter was no random chance; The Onyx had meticulously observed the daily routines of their potential victims, calculating with precision the exact moment she would arrive at the shop.

The woman, appearing to be in her mid-twenties and displaying a timid demeanour, headed to the shop to purchase some drinks for her nearby home. Her destination was just around the corner, and her shopping list included two large bottles of Fanta and a bottle of Coke. After completing her purchase and settling the bill, she exited the store, leaving the tired shop worker to prepare for closing time. It was now ten-thirty-five PM, and the town remained as desolate as ever.

As she walked out, she had to pass by The Onyx once more, unbeknownst to her that they were lurking at the side of the shop. Turning the corner, she became the target of The Onyx's sudden attack. Swiftly, they seized her, their arms tightening around her neck, causing her to drop the bag containing the drinks onto the roadside.

In a desperate bid to break free, the woman fought back, forcefully driving her head backward into The Onyx's chin, forcing them to release their grip. She began to flee, screams for help escaping her lips, knowing that her house was just a two-minute sprint away from the shop. However, The Onyx, with their exceptional athleticism, rapidly closed the distance, striking her in the back of the head with a brick.

Her body slammed to the ground, blood oozing from her wounded skull. In this gruesome moment, there were no witnesses in sight. Then, suddenly, a beam of light pierced the darkness as a car approached, about to turn the corner. The Onyx, recognising the danger of exposure, hastily retreated from the scene, leaving behind the bloodied brick and the lifeless body.

The approaching car, driven by a male, made the turn, its driver initially unaware of the horrifying scene before him. As the realisation dawned, his eyes filled with fear and dread. Who was this driving?

As my gruelling overtime shift at Glaze Cafe finally came to an end, the pulsating rhythm of music in my car seemed feeble in its attempt to uplift my spirits. Happiness eluded me once again. Weary from work, I embarked on my journey home, the need to earn every hard-earned pound serving as my relentless motivation.

As I navigated the familiar route, taking the corner that marked a mere ten-minute stretch from my humble abode, my eyes caught something inexplicable. I couldn't believe my initial thoughts, dismissing them as preposterous.

"No, this can't be real," I murmured to myself, my chest constricting with anxiety, and my heart pounding frantically. At first glance, it seemed like there was a dead body on the street.

Unable to ignore the dreadful possibility, I parked my car with trembling hands. The world around me seemed engulfed in darkness, amplifying my apprehension. As I cautiously approached the ominous sight, I held on to a glimmer of hope that my fears would be disproved. Yet, my worst apprehensions were confirmed: a lifeless body lay before me.

It was not just any lifeless body, but one I recognised all too well— my dad's former girlfriend, the woman he dated briefly after parting ways with my mum. Their relationship had barely spanned two months. The sinister connection to my father, James Senior, intensified the distressing implications of this discovery. I couldn't bear the weight of it all.

Panic surged through me, and instinctively, I retreated to my car, my mind a whirlwind of anxiety and self-reproach. What had I done? I had become an unwitting witness to a murder, the victim lying lifeless right before my eyes. Yet, I had fled, succumbing to fear and indecision.

But a fierce determination overcame me, and I made a life-altering decision. I turned back to the corner shop, the gravity of the situation outweighing my fear. I had to act. I scanned the dimly lit surroundings, desperately searching for any sign of the perpetrator. However, the obscurity of the night concealed their presence, and I remained oblivious to their whereabouts.

With mounting unease, I realised that the killer could have vanished into the shadows by now, leaving no trace of their escape. My sense of urgency grew, but my efforts were in vain. I saw nothing. I had no idea how long the lifeless body had lain there, or when the brutal act had occurred.

Reluctantly, I summoned the authorities, my voice quivering as I reported my gruesome discovery. The fear of suspicion gnawed at me—my connection to the victim, the bloodied brick nearby, all raised unsettling questions. All I could do was recount the truth, hoping that it would be enough to absolve me of any wrongdoing.

My father's impending court date loomed on the horizon, and I couldn't afford to be entangled in this chilling web of events.

I found myself back at the police station, a mere day away from my father's impending court trial. The weight of the recent events hung heavily over me. I couldn't help but wonder why fate had chosen me to stumble upon that lifeless body. The hours ahead promised to be arduous.

Inside the station, I was directed to a room where Officer Bellis awaited me. It was the same officer I had encountered during my father's case, and his imposing presence always left me feeling vulnerable, as though he possessed the uncanny ability to peer into my thoughts. His hands, large and strong like those of a gorilla, held the secrets to countless cases involving my family's tragic murders.

He sat across from me in silence, a stack of papers placed face down on the table between us, obscuring their contents from view. Then, with a heavy sigh, Officer Bellis raised his gaze to meet mine.

"Back here again, are we, James?" he inquired, his tone tinged with an air of knowing.

I couldn't deny the discomfort that his presence invoked.

"I suppose so," I replied, my reluctance palpable.

"I didn't choose to be here, though."

"Why is that, I wonder?" Officer Bellis continued, his words carrying an insinuation that pierced through me.

It was as though he believed I held knowledge about the identity of the woman's murderer. My posture stiffened.

"Pardon me?" I responded, seeking clarification.

"What were your actions when you stumbled upon the body, James?" Officer Bellis inquired, his piercing gaze unwavering.

"I immediately called the police," I answered, opting for a version of the truth. However, I knew that my response was not entirely accurate.

"Immediately?" Officer Bellis pressed, his scepticism apparent.

"Yes," I affirmed, despite the knowledge that this was my first untruth during the police interview. I hope Officer Bellis believes me. After all, what harm could a small lie do?

With deliberate intent, Officer Bellis turned over the stack of papers, revealing their contents to both of us.

"So, are you telling me that this isn't you here... and here?" he asked, his voice carrying a weight of accusation, as he pointed to two distinct timestamps on the documents.

I found myself in a precarious position. The all-seeing CCTV camera had captured my actions-both driving away and returning to the scene. The police had instant access to every camera, within minutes. My heart sank as I examined the incriminating images, their timestamps clearly marking the sequence of events. There was no plausible explanation that could redeem me, but I mustered the courage to offer an account of my actions.

"Yes, that's me," I admitted,

"I panicked; I was completely lost in the moment, not knowing how to react." My voice laced with regret

Officer Bellis continued to scrutinise me.

"So, you chose to leave a deceased body on the side of the road," he pressed, his words heavy with accusation.

"You suspected she might be dead, didn't you, James?"

"No, not exactly," I stammered, attempting to clarify.

"I mean, I had a sinking feeling when I first saw her, but I couldn't bring myself to accept it. The shock overwhelmed me, and I thought I was going to have a heart attack. I couldn't bear to look at her, and it was my first encounter with a dead body. I didn't know how to react."

"Then why did you return?" Officer Bellis probed further.

"Because I wanted to do the right thing," I explained earnestly.

"I began to fear that someone out there might be targeting people my father cared about. I thought the perpetrator might still be nearby. That's why I rushed back to the scene."

Officer Bellis maintained his stoic demeanour, but I could sense a shift in his disposition. Relief washed over me as it seemed he was beginning to believe my account. Thank goodness for small mercies. I couldn't help but wonder why I hadn't chosen honesty from the outset.

As the interview concluded, Officer Bellis released me from the room. Exiting, I spotted a familiar face at a distance, undergoing questioning by the police. My heart raced as I tried to get a better view before leaving the police station.

Drawing closer, the familiar visage became unmistakable-it was Shannon, my sister, engaged in a conversation with the authorities. My mind reeled in disbelief. What could have brought her to this place? I hesitated for a moment, my confusion and concern mounting, before ultimately deciding to approach her.

Shannon glanced up, our eyes locking briefly in surprise before she hastily averted her gaze.

"Shannon?" I uttered her name softly, my voice laden with a mixture of astonishment and anxiety.

She turned her gaze back to me, her countenance betraying a medley of emotions-surprise, guilt, and possibly fear.

"James? What are you doing here?"

I returned her question, my concern growing.

"I could ask you the same thing. Why are you here? What's happening?"

She hesitated, casting a wary glance around as if searching for the right words.

"It's... it's nothing, really. Just some inquiries about... well, about Dad."

"Dad?" I furrowed my brow, struggling to grasp the situation.

"Why would they be questioning you about Dad?"

Shannon appeared uncomfortable, avoiding my eyes.

"They're just... they're looking into things, James. Trying to piece together the puzzle. You know how it is."

I nodded, though the enigma persisted.

"But what does this have to do with you?" I asked.

She sighed, as if grappling with her response.

"They think I might have information related to these recent murders. Murders that somehow seem to be tied to Dad."

My heart quickened, a heavy foreboding settling within me. The notion that these murders were connected to our father was deeply unsettling.

"Do you? Have any information, I mean?"

Shannon's eyes darted, and for a fleeting moment, I sensed more than guilt in her gaze-fear, perhaps.

"No, James, I don't. I hardly even saw Dad after he left. You know that."

Her words made sense, but a disquiet lingered in her tone, one I couldn't ignore.

"Shan, if there's something you're not telling me-"

"Listen, James, I can't discuss this right now," she interjected, her voice strained.

"I just... I need to handle this on my own, okay?"

I wanted to press further, to unearth the truth behind her unease, but her plea was genuine. It was clear she was genuinely apprehensive. Reluctantly, I nodded.

"Alright, but if you need anything..."

She mustered a faint, forced smile. "Thanks, James. I'll manage."

We exchanged a meaningful glance, and then she redirected her attention to the officer. I left the police station, my thoughts consumed by a whirlwind of questions and anxieties. The realisation that Shannon was somehow entangled in this enigma added an intricate layer to an already complex situation.

With my father's impending court date looming, I was already grappling with an overwhelming burden. Now, it seemed our family was ensnared in something far more ominous and perilous than I had ever imagined. As I made my way home, a nagging feeling persisted, as though I stood on the precipice of uncovering a revelation that could reshape everything.

CHAPTER 9

The day of James Senior.'s court trial had arrived, and the story had become a global sensation, dominating headlines worldwide. The once-quiet town of Emberglade was now at the centre of a sensational case involving a notorious killer.

Two prominent lawyers had been chosen to represent James Senior, while equally skilled attorneys stood for Layla's grieving family. The pressure surrounding this case was immense, with thousands of people closely following each development.

Outside the courtroom, the persistent mobs in Emberglade's streets continued their protests, demanding justice and the imprisonment of the accused. Inside, the courtroom's public gallery filled up quickly, with faces both familiar and new.

The Jones family members were present, though their mother was notably absent. Luton, and Alfie, the two men who had initiated the mob, occupied opposite ends of the room.

Layla's family, which included her father, mother, and cousins, was in attendance. Officer Bellis and Terry sat alone, solemn observers. James Junior's boss was also present.

Mister. Foster was diligently preparing James Senior. for the gruelling trial ahead, subjecting him to a barrage of tough questions to simulate the intense courtroom environment.

This rigorous training aimed to familiarise James Senior with the harsh scrutiny he would face and to assess his responses, including any telltale signs of dishonesty. Mr. Foster understood that any missteps during the trial could be detrimental to his client's chances of acquittal.

This was a crucial moment for James Senior as he would soon come face-to-face with his family for the first time since the alleged murder.

He needed to maintain his composure, concealing his emotions from both the jury and his loved ones. The jury had been meticulously selected, and the trial was poised to commence, with the weight of his future hanging in the balance.

As James Senior entered the courtroom, he purposefully averted his gaze, avoiding eye contact with anyone present. The palpable emotions radiating from Layla's family were etched on their faces as they observed his entrance.

James Junior yearned to connect with his father through eye contact, but the opportunity slipped away like sand through his fingers.

Initially, James Senior. slouched in his chair, prompting a discreet but firm reminder from his lawyer to maintain an upright posture. He understood the importance of leaving a favourable impression on both the judge and the jury, and he promptly corrected his posture.

Mrs. Samantha Mitchell, representing Layla's family, bore the weight of the case alone, recognising that her family's emotions were too overwhelming to endure the spotlight. Nevertheless, they understood the necessity of testifying for their cause.

The looming question revolved around the sufficiency of the available CCTV footage as evidence.

"Your Honour, I respectfully request to summon Darius as a witness," Mitchell implored, calling upon Layla's father to take the stand.

Anxious but resolute, he made his way to the witness stand, acknowledging his discomfort with public speaking while remaining steadfast in his determination to speak about his late daughter before the assembled audience.

"Could you please share your relationship and history with both Layla and James Senior?" Mitchell inquired gently.

"I am Layla's father," Darius began, his voice steady despite the turbulent emotions beneath the surface.

"She was in a relationship with this man for a year, and I had the opportunity to become well-acquainted with him during that time."

"What can you tell us about James Senior?" Mitchell inquired.

"He's a terrible, emotionally abusive man who subjected her to daily torment, and he's a murderer!" Darius replied vehemently.

"OBJECTION, YOUR HONOUR! Speculation, hearsay," Foster interjected.

"Sustained," the judge responded, dismissing Darius's response.

Mitchell continued with her questioning, delving into the distressing experiences that Darius had personally witnessed between Layla and James Senior.

Although Foster objected again, Mitchell clarified that Darius was recounting his own firsthand observations. She successfully established that Darius had witnessed James Senior. physically abusing Layla.

"In your professional opinion, do you believe this man is capable of causing harm to Layla?" Mitchell asked, her voice filled with empathy.

"I do," Darius affirmed solemnly.

"Why would your daughter not tell you this?" Mitchell questioned.

"She loved him, as much as I hated that man. She had double the love for James." Darius had raw emotion on his face, letting his heart out on the stand.

"I can see how much this man has hurt your family. How have you all been dealing with her loss?" Mitchell knew exactly what questions to ask to get sympathy from the Jury.

"We're broken..." Darius paused and tried to catch his breath, full of tears, rage made him unable to speak.

He waited a few minutes to calm himself and proceeded to answer the question.

"No one will understand the feeling of losing your child. You bring them into this world, and they make your life a better place. She made me happy every single day. The day she was murdered, my happiness has gone. The knife also went through my heart mentally. This man deserves to be in prison for life."

Mitchell handed Darius more tissues, but she got the answers that she wanted from him.

"No further questions, Your Honour," Mitchell concluded.

The jury diligently took notes, clearly affected by Darius's emotional testimony, which had left a profound impact. In contrast, James Senior. appeared emotionally detached during his own testimony, displaying little interest in the ongoing proceedings. Now, it was Foster's turn to cross-examine the grieving father.

"Darius Smith, you loved Layla, didn't you?" Foster inquired.

"Of course, I did, and I still do. She's my only daughter," Darius replied with a hint of defensiveness.

"Then why did you only visit her once every few months?" Foster probed.

"That's not true," Darius retorted.

"Your Honour, I'd like to introduce Exhibit forty-five, which contains text messages from Mr. Smith," Mitchell interjected, her surprise evident as he presented this unexpected evidence.

"May we approach, Your Honour?" Both attorneys approached the judge to discuss the unexpected evidence. Layla's legal team felt taken aback by this late addition, while Foster argued that the evidence had been obtained recently and was vital to the case.

The judge allowed the evidence but reminded Foster to present evidence in a more timely manner. The trial resumed, with Foster continuing his questioning of Darius.

"As you can see, Darius Smith and Layla Smith exchanged text messages. Layla wrote,

'I miss you, dad. It's been two months. I want to see you.'

which Darius responded,

'I have a life, Layla. I'm working and then spending time with your mother. You're a grown-up now.'

Layla replied with a crying emoji, and Darius added,

'I'll try to see you next month.'

Foster proceeded to the next set of texts, which occurred two months after the previous exchange.

'I guess you don't want to see me then,' Layla expressed her frustration."

Foster then turned off the texts on the screen.

"Mister. Smith, can you please explain why you didn't try to visit your daughter during this time?" Foster asked, his tone probing.

Darius, his emotions still raw from the previous questions, responded,

"It was a difficult time for me. I was struggling financially."

"So, it is true that you didn't visit their house for four months?" Foster pressed.

Darius hesitated before answering,

"Yes, but I used to visit frequently before that. I loved spending time with Layla. That man was terrible to her. He wouldn't let her see me."

The attorney continued,

"You claim to have witnessed Mister. Jones hitting your daughter?"

"Yes, I've seen it multiple times," Darius affirmed.

"Then wouldn't you be concerned and visit your daughter, who was living with and spending all her time with this man?" Foster questioned further.

"I wanted to, I just couldn't," Darius replied, his voice filled with remorse.

Foster continued his line of questioning, stating, "You clearly didn't try hard enough, did you, Mister. Smith?"

At this point, Mitchell interjected,

"Objection, Your Honour, leading!"

Foster concluded his cross-examination with,

"No more questions, Your Honour."

Foster kept it short and sweet, attempting to portray Darius as a liar and a bad father.

Darius, visibly shaken, left the witness stand, feeling emotionally drained. It had been one of the most challenging experiences of his life. However, there was one more witness to testify today, this time from James Junior.'s side.

In most courts around the world, there is a standard practice where each team has a designated day for testifying, and they choose which witnesses will take the stand. However, Emberglade operates differently.

In Emberglade, each team calls up their witnesses one by one, taking turns in the order they prefer.

Foster stood up to announce the next witness.

"Your Honour, I would like to call Selena Jones to the witness stand," he declared.

James Junior and Shannon were surprised, as they hadn't been informed that Selena, their sister, would be testifying.

Selena approached the stand with an unusual air of confidence. Her typically timid demeanour seemed to have been replaced with newfound strength. Though speaking in public was usually intimidating for her, she appeared determined to speak on behalf of her father.

"Hello, Selena. Can you describe your relationship with your father?" Foster initiated the questioning.

"It wasn't perfect. Honestly, we don't see each other as much as I'd like. But we exchange texts every few days and occasionally talk on the phone," Selena responded.

"How would you characterise your father's personality?" Foster inquired.

"He's kind, loving, and respectful to everyone. He worked hard to provide for Layla," Selena replied.

"Did you ever witness him mistreat Layla physically?" Foster asked.

"Never," Selena replied firmly.

"Have you seen him become aggressive with Layla?" Foster questioned.

"I haven't," Selena maintained.

Foster pressed further,

"Have you ever heard him speak harshly to Layla?" This was part of his strategy to respond to Layla's team's questions in a more confrontational manner.

"No, he loved Layla. While I didn't want him and my mother to split, he cared for her," Selena answered.

"So would you say your family liked Layla"

"Yes, she was lovely to us and we always showed her respect. We loved Layla." Selena was constantly pulling on her trousers to help with her confidence.

"For my final question, Mrs Jones, do you believe your father is innocent?" Foster inquired.

"I wholeheartedly believe he's innocent. This man has never laid a finger on any of his children, let alone any woman," Selena affirmed.

Foster concluded his questioning, portraying Layla as an honest, caring daughter who perceived her father in a positive light. The jury remained neutral, but their satisfaction with the testimony was evident.

Now it was Mitchell's turn to cross-examine Selena.

"Mrs. Jones, you mentioned that you weren't happy about your father's separation from your mother, correct?" Mitchell began.

"Yes, anyone would be upset by their parents' breakup," Selena acknowledged.

"This would make you angry and lead you to stop seeing your father, wouldn't it?" Mitchell probed.

"I wouldn't say angry, but I was hurt. Seeing my mother upset made me feel like I had to choose a side," Selena explained.

"You would encourage your father to reconcile with your mother, wouldn't you?" Mitchell continued.

"Objection! Calls for speculation," Mister. Foster objected firmly.

The judge sustained the objection, prompting Mrs Mitchell to rephrase the question.

"Did you tell your father that you missed your parents being together?" Mitchell asked.

"No, I didn't," Selena replied.

"This hurt you, didn't it? You felt upset and hurt. You placed this pressure on your father, didn't you?" Mitchell inquired.

"I... um..." Selena hesitated, getting frustrated with the constant barrage of accusations.

"That's how it began, with your father feeling rejected and angry. How do you think he vented that anger, Mrs. Jones?" Mitchell pressed further.

"I don't know. He's not an angry person. He loves Layla," Selena responded.

"Do you believe he directed his anger at Layla when he returned home?" Mitchell questioned.

"No, I don't!" Selena vehemently denied.

"Then how do you explain the bruises?" Mitchell challenged. Showing the evidence of it for the first time to the jury.

"I don't know," Selena admitted.

"You don't know? So, Mrs. Jones, you're saying you don't know how he behaves. The truth is, you no longer know this man, do you?" Mitchell asserted.

"He's my father! I know him, okay? I know him!" Selena's composure wavered, and she raised her voice in frustration.

"All of you were hurting, wanting your parents to reunite. Your father still loved your mother, didn't he?" Mitchell continued to press.

Selena hesitated, her gaze shifting between the jury and her father.

"Answer the question, Mrs. Jones. Did your father still love your mother?" Mitchell insisted.

"Yes," Selena finally admitted.

"That's correct. So, we've established that both you and your father were hurt, angry, and wanting your family back together. But Layla stood in the way, didn't she?" Mitchell concluded.

"No, it's not like that!" Selena protested.

"No further questions, Your Honour," Mitchell concluded.

Selena raised from her seat and continued to defend her father passionately, attempting to paint a positive image. However, her outburst only annoyed the judge, who instructed her to return to her seat, emphasising the need to maintain decorum in the courtroom. This marked a significant day in the James Senior and Layla Smith case, with the verdict inching closer.

CHAPTER 10

The trial drew to a dramatic close, marked by its fair share of heated arguments and raised voices. As the proceedings concluded, it was time for everyone to make their way home.

On their exit from the courtroom, Luton and Alfie found themselves crossing paths, both keenly aware that starting a fight in the presence of the police would be unwise. Approaching each other cautiously, Alfie made an effort to extend an olive branch.

"Listen, I'm not here to stir up trouble. I want to apologise for the beating I gave you. We both cared about Layla, right?" Alfie attempted a conciliatory tone.

Luton's expression twisted with disdain as Alfie spoke.

"I still have these black eyes because of you. Your apology means nothing. You have no idea how much I cared for Layla."

"You've got some serious issues, you know that?" Alfie retorted, growing frustrated.

"Don't come near me again, or I'll contact people who can put you in a wheelchair like your brother," Luton threatened coldly.

Alfie was incensed by this comment and felt the urge to throw another punch at Luton. However, he hesitated, reconsidering his actions as Officer Bellis watched closely.

Alfie ultimately chose not to act, a wise decision given the presence of law enforcement. But the question lingered: Why was Officer Bellis there? He wasn't on duty and had arrived of his own accord.

The circumstances seemed peculiar for a police officer. James Junior. also found this situation odd and was struck by a curious thought upon returning home.

Returning home from the courthouse alongside his two sisters, James Junior remained in a state of shock following Selena's unexpected support for their father. Selena's involvement had taken him by surprise, as she typically shied away from public situations.

While he admired her bravery, he couldn't help but think that she shouldn't have placed herself in such a precarious position. After all, none of them were certain whether their father was guilty or innocent.

As he reflected on the trial, James Junior. recalled the presence of numerous familiar faces in the courtroom. Many of them harboured animosity towards his father or had some form of connection to him.

Could the killer be among them? Could it be Onyx? The idea didn't seem implausible. Onyx appeared to have an unhealthy fixation on his father, and given the depth of their obsession, they could very well have been present at the trial.

As his thoughts continued to evolve, Junior.'s mind wandered into unsettling territory. What if the killer was someone he knew, even someone within his own family? His sister Shannon, who held a deep grudge against their father, had been questioned at the police station alone.

Could she possibly be a suspect? The uncertainty weighed heavily on James Junior, leaving him overwhelmed with the suspicion that the murderer might be someone close to him.

Determined to investigate further, Junior approaches Shannon, hoping to discern any telling reactions from her. He engages her in casual conversation, taking note of her evident weariness after the lengthy trial.

She vents her frustration regarding Selena's decision to testify, deeming it detrimental to their father's case. However, when Junior probes whether Selena had informed her of this choice beforehand, Shannon's demeanour undergoes a noticeable shift.

She avoids making eye contact, begins to absentmindedly scratch herself, and fidgets restlessly. Her behaviour raises suspicions.

"Are you listening, Shan?" James inquired.

"Yes, Junior, but I'm so tired of talking about the trial and murders. It's terrifying and unnerves me. I really don't want to discuss it anymore. Please, let's stop," Shannon responds.

Junior decided to stop questioning his sister but remained committed to his quest to uncover the identity of the Emberglade murderer, the elusive Onyx.

Alfie was preoccupied with gathering supplies for his mob, with the intention of fuelling further unrest in town. The vulnerability of his brother drove him to expedite his errands and return home promptly.

However, upon arriving at his house, Alfie was met with an unsettling sight. The front door was unlocked, and the house was eerily empty. Panic surged through him as he realised that his brother Joel was missing and no sign of his carer.

Given his physical limitations, his brother couldn't have left on his own accord. Alfie's anxiety escalated, and he feared the worst – had his brother been abducted or harmed? Or worse, could Alfie himself be somehow involved in his brother's disappearance?

The escalating chaos in Emberglade and the looming presence of Onyx only intensified the tension. The transformation of the once-quiet and obscure town into a murder-stricken community under global scrutiny underscored the gravity of the situation.

As the night wore on, Alfie embarked on an increasingly frantic search for his missing brother. He navigated through dimly lit alleys and deserted streets, his heart pounding with anxiety at every step.

At the same time, James Junior found himself consumed by suspicions regarding his own family's potential involvement in the murders, driving him relentlessly to unearth the truth.

Little did they know, another sinister chapter in the Emberglade saga was unfolding, drawing them inexorably closer to the heart of the town's dark and twisted secrets.

CHAPTER 11

On the day of the most recent murder, the mysterious killer known as Onyx once again donned their dark grey and black attire, maintaining their enigmatic presence. As people began to speculate about each person's whereabouts on that ominous night, a puzzling pattern emerged.

James Senior was behind bars during the investigation, James Junior was away from home, and Shannon was also absent. Selena and her mother had remained together in their residence. Luton and Alfie were notably missing from their homes.

The fact that all potential suspects were out of their homes at the time of the murder only deepened the mystery surrounding the identity of the perpetrator.

Junior found himself wrestling with a flood of emotions once more, leading him to schedule another therapy session with Oliver.

While their previous sessions had been helpful, the last one had left James intrigued by Oliver's unorthodox approach. Some might consider it unprofessional, but James appreciated the need for a unique method given his unusual circumstances.

He preferred this approach over a clinical and robotic one.

As James entered the therapist's office, he couldn't help but notice that the usually impeccable room appeared slightly dishevelled. Nonetheless, he took a seat, ready to release the pent-up frustration that had been building inside him.

"ARGHHHHH!" Junior suddenly screamed at the top of his lungs, catching Oliver off guard.

In response, Oliver calmly remarked,

"That was unexpected." He chuckles.

"Sometimes, venting through screaming can be a helpful way to calm the mind."

Apologising, James confides,

"I've been holding onto a lot of rage, and I feel emotionally exposed around you."

Oliver responds with a reassuring smile, saying,

"It's okay. I'm glad you trust me. What's been troubling you lately?"

James begins to unload his concerns, stating,

"What haven't I dealt with? I'm stuck in the same situation where I don't know if my father is guilty, and I have no idea who the murderer is. It could be anyone. I..."

Suddenly, James notices a dark grey jacket, interrupting himself with an anxious tone.

"Is that your jacket?" His voice quivered.

Oliver turns to look, his expression marked by confusion, as he wonders why James is so fixated on his jacket.

"Yes, it is. Why do you ask?"

"The Onyx, they wear dark grey and black," James rose from his seat, his anxiety intensifying as the troubling thought surfaces.

"James, you're going through a lot right now. Please, just sit down," Oliver implores, sensing James's distress.

"No! Is it you? Tell me, tell me if it's you!" James's voice trembles with fear as he grapples with the overwhelming suspicion that has suddenly taken hold of him.

Maintaining his calm demeanour, Oliver responds,

"I've had this coat the entire time, James. It's just a normal grey coat. Please, sit down. I want to help you."

As James recollects the room's appearance, he remembers that the grey jacket was indeed present all along and slowly takes a seat.

Perhaps it's just an ordinary jacket, he thinks. Hundreds of people in Emberglade likely own a similar grey jacket. The notion, however, hurts him. He thought Oliver was the one person he could trust. While he sits down again, uncertainty fills him.

Oliver addresses the situation, saying,

"James, I don't want you feeling this way around me. I genuinely want to help. But if you're losing your grip to the point where you believe I could be a killer, maybe you should consider finding a new therapist."

"No, no, I'm sorry. I overreacted. I own a grey jacket myself. I don't know why it just startled me for a moment."

"Are you sure you can continue?" Oliver inquires.

"Yes, but can I see the jacket?" James asks.

Without hesitation, Oliver hands over the jacket. James inspects it closely, searching for any marks, notes, or blood. However, he finds nothing. It becomes evident that he's overreacted due to his overwhelming emotions.

Oliver, a compassionate man aiming to aid someone going through a difficult time, reassures James. He recognises that his reputation as a therapist is at stake, especially considering the media's attention on the case.

After apologising and leaving the therapist's office, James grappled with the possibility of losing his only confidant due to his own paranoia. Although his initial plan was to head home, he made a decision to embark on a quest to track down Onyx.

Despite harbouring suspicions about his therapist, he acknowledges the unlikelihood of Oliver being the killer. Nevertheless, he remains vigilant.

With a clear destination in mind, on his search for the Onyx. Junior proceeds to Luton's house to check if he's present. The house is veiled in darkness, casting an eerie ambiance. Junior knocks, waits, and methodically scans his surroundings, but there is no response.

He curiously checks under the doormat and discovers a key, prompting him to wonder why so many in Emberglade leave keys in such an easily accessible spot. Succumbing to his urgency, Junior unlocks the door, feeling a twinge of unease as he acts entirely out of character, resorting to breaking and entering.

He cautiously explores Luton's personal effects, discretely searching for any evidence that could link him to Onyx.

His attention is drawn to a grey jacket hanging up, sowing doubt about whether it's merely a common article of clothing or part of the Onyx attire. The ambiguity deepens, further complicating James's quest to distinguish between the two.

Suddenly, a door slams shut, jolting him with fear and signalling Luton's return home. Caught between Luton and potential danger, Junior realises the grave risks he's taking by being there.

With a sense of urgency, he silently navigates his way downstairs, hoping to elude Luton, who now wields a sharp knife, likely for self-defence If he spots the intruder.

As Junior approaches a pivotal juncture with the kitchen on his left and the staircase on his right, he anxiously hopes that Luton won't abruptly turn around. He manages to slip past the kitchen without incident and, with bated breath, quietly heads toward the back door, intending to make his exit without being noticed.

However, the door made a substantial noise when it closed. Fearing that Luton might have heard it, James hesitated and turned back to check. Unfortunately, Luton did indeed hear the sound.

The slam prompted Luton to react impulsively, causing him to accidentally cut his thumb, which led to a gush of blood pouring from the wound. He swiftly wrapped his thumb in a nearby towel, clutching the knife tightly in his other hand, ready to confront any potential threat.

As Luton cautiously opened the front door, all he managed to glimpse was Junior's leg as he sprinted around the corner. In his heightened state of alertness, Luton chose not to chase. Instead, he locked the door firmly and immediately dialled the police.

"Someone's just been in my house! I saw his leg. I think I know who it was," Luton urgently informed the operator.

"Okay, sir, try to stay calm. Who do you think it was?" the operator inquired.

"Alfie... he's been out to get me for ages. You've got to help me," Luton responded frantically.

"Police are on their way, they won't be long," the operator assured him.

Unbeknownst to Luton, he had mistaken James Junior for Alfie, which could potentially cause significant confusion for the arriving police officers.

They were already under immense pressure to apprehend the Emberglade murderer, and this unexpected distraction wasn't aiding their efforts.

However, what Luton didn't realise was that the police had intended to visit his house regardless, as they believed they might uncover crucial evidence related to the two murders. They had strong suspicions that he could be the Onyx.

"Police, open up!" came the authoritative command at Luton's door.

After impatiently waiting for nearly twenty minutes, Luton opened the door with frustration etched on his face, believing that the police were there to offer assistance. Unfortunately, his assumptions were mistaken.

"You're under arrest on suspicion of committing the two murders," declared one of the police officers.

"Are you taking the piss? You're here to help me, not come up with false accusations," Luton retorted, bewildered by the unexpected turn of events.

Luton resisted arrest, and as a result, he was forcefully wrestled to the ground. He still had his black eye, which had not fully healed, now had additional bruises along his arms. His pleas about the intruder in his house fell on deaf ears, as the police remained resolute in their mission.

Luton's deep love for Layla, coupled with his inability to accept her tragic demise and the continued freedom of her killer, had driven him to lash out at Layla's former lovers in a misguided attempt to find justice.

It was unclear whether his rage would have extended to targeting James Senior.'s family next. All that was certain at that moment was that Luton, the alleged Onyx Emberglade Killer, had been apprehended by the authorities.

CHAPTER 12

The news of the alleged 'Emberglade killer' being captured quickly spread throughout the entire town. While many families felt a sense of relief, the pervasive fear of not knowing if they could become the next target still lingered, especially for the Jones family.

With the murders all linked to James Senior, the uncertainty weighed heavily on their minds.

However, one person did not share in the town's collective relief: James Junior. He had been inside Luton's house on the night of the arrest, meticulously searching every corner, and he couldn't bring himself to believe that Luton was the true killer.

Nevertheless, the evidence gathered by the police seemed to tell a different story. The public are unsure on what this evidence may be.

Lots of Thoughts were on James mind. Perhaps the police had already been there, he thought.

All he could do now was wait and see how the police investigation unfolded, acknowledging the possibility that he might have been wrong.

"Junior!" His mother's voice calling them down for dinner which interrupted his thoughts.

Mealtime was one of the few occasions when the family gathered together. James noticed the toll the ongoing crisis had taken on his mother.

She had lost a significant amount of weight and appeared unhealthy. Tessa struggled to eat, often subsisting on just a piece of toast and a coffee throughout the day. Concern for her well-being weighed heavily on Junior, especially with Shannon still in the house.

Though he felt guilty for entertaining such thoughts, he couldn't deny the growing apprehension he had about Shannon. Having a potential murderer in the same household, and as a sibling no less, was a terrifying notion.

James knew he couldn't confront her until he had concrete evidence, not only to protect himself but also to safeguard his family from the looming uncertainty.

"You doing alright, James? You seem a bit on edge," Shannon inquires.

"Yeah, I'm fine. Don't sweat it," I reply.

"Don't worry, I won't." She smirks.

Usually, their playful banter would be amusing, but now, he can't help but wonder if she's being sincere. Thank goodness I've got a lock on my bedroom door, he thought.

Selena glances at my mother.

"You really should eat more; I'm getting concerned."

"Don't be ridiculous, Selena, I eat just fine," my mum retorts.

"Toast doesn't count." Selena replied.

"Well, is anyone planning to cook for once? You're all grown-ups, and I'm still the one doing everything. Don't you think I have enough going on right now; I don't need to stress about meals being late." Tessa snaps.

They all exchanged glances, the three of them taken aback by her sudden outburst. It's evident that their mother is on the verge of breaking down. She's going through just as much, if not more, than the rest of them.

Maybe she needs to consider seeing a therapist? As for Junior, he still hasn't had a chance to speak to his therapist. Oliver. since their last session. He really wishes he could still just meet up with him, but he won't return his calls. Right now, he feels like he has no one to confide in; there's no one who will truly listen to Junior if he decides to open up.

He finds it difficult to trust anyone completely. Some things are best kept to himself he believes. For instance, James can't share the fact that he broke into Luton's house; that could have led to his arrest and made him look incredibly suspicious, especially considering everything that's happening.

93

Today, I've decided to take a break and treat myself to a meal at Glaze Cafe, where I work. I haven't been working many shifts lately due to everything that's been happening and the public backlash I've been facing. However, I'm hoping that my colleagues will be happy to see me.

As I hop In my car and make my way, I once again come across that large mob that seems to be out there every single day.

It's been a constant source of distress. They even got close to our house once, and someone attempted to throw a brick through our window. Fortunately, we have some kind-hearted neighbours who somehow managed to convince them otherwise.

In the midst of this crowd, I notice a few familiar faces, but one stands out to me, and it's the first time I've seen them in the mob. It's Terry, a coworker from my workplace.

It's baffling to see him there, screaming for my family to face harm or imprisonment.

We've worked together for years, and I've always been friendly to him. But if he ever ends up on the same shift with me again, I might just lose my job because the urge to confront him is growing stronger by the day.

I arrive at the cafe, and as expected, all eyes turn to stare at me. I've grown accustomed to this daily routine of being the centre of attention, and honestly, I've just learned to ignore it.

I place my order, opting for my favourite meal, an all-day breakfast, and I go big, ordering an extra-large portion. My mum's cooking has taken a hit as she struggles to find the energy to put into her meals.

As the waiter brings over my food and starts arranging it on my plate, an infuriating incident occurs. Out of nowhere, some random man approaches and spits in my food. My immediate reaction is to jump to my feet, ready for a confrontation.

The waiter, however, intervenes, restraining the man and shouting at me to leave our town, accusing me of being worse than my father, a murderer. It's a statement that cuts deep, and I'm just about fed up with these constant troubles. It feels like I might need a bodyguard at this. I just thought he wanted a reaction out of me. But once again, no one comes to my defence, other than my manager. Thankfully, he ushers him out of the restaurant.

The waiter takes my food away and returns with a fresh, untouched meal. I decided to take my time and savour the delicious food; there's no rush to head back home and dwell on life's difficulties. Instead, I'll remain here, enjoying my meal, and keeping to myself.

The cafe door swings open, and I hear my manager's voice. "Getting ready for your shift?" he asks.

I turn around to identify the speaker, and to my surprise, it's Terry.

I've already caused quite a bit of trouble at this cafe, and I can't continue to create disruptions, even though I'm tempted to. Terry, who used to claim he was a friend, has changed everything by appearing on the streets and demanding my downfall.

Terry glances in my direction, his face contorted with anger as he realises it's me. I see him whisper something to our manager, and they both turn to face me. Fortunately, I'm just finishing up my meal.

Terry approaches to clear my plate. "All done, mate?" he asks, attempting to strike up a conversation in a friendlier tone.

"Obviously," I reply with a hint of sarcasm.

Terry, however, takes things to a shocking extreme. He grabs the half-full glass of coke and pours it all over my face, then attempts to hurl the glass at my head. Reacting swiftly, I throw myself to the floor to avoid the glass projectile.

My heart races as he then seizes the knife I had just used for my meal and swings it menacingly in my direction. The knife lands perilously close between my legs, and in a desperate bid to disarm him, I kick his arm, causing him to drop the weapon.

With a surge of adrenaline, I deliver a powerful right-hand punch to the side of Terry's head, causing him to collapse. Without looking back, I made a run for it.

To my disbelief, the entire cafe rushes to Terry's aid. It's baffling; here I am, the target of a vicious attack, and yet he's the one receiving assistance. It's become increasingly evident that this town is truly out to get me.

As I'm in the midst of running away, I try to reflect on my life. I find it hard to put into words. It's as though I'm trapped in a surreal movie or a work of fiction, detached from reality. But I'm undeniably real, and my life has taken a nightmarish turn.

It's disconcerting how swiftly people have turned against me. Not too long ago, I was well-liked by everyone in this town. The rapid change is unnerving.

Tomorrow, my father's court case begins, but I'm still traumatised by what transpired at the cafe. I'm not sure if I'll have the strength to attend court; I'll make that decision on the day.

Images of the cafe incident keep haunting me. When I was sprawled on the floor, with Terry wielding a knife over me, I had a chilling vision of my father in the same menacing stance. In that moment, I felt what it must have been like for Layla.

It was a terrifying experience. Part of me considered just accepting the knife to the chest and enduring this torment daily. It's taking a toll on my mental and physical well-being, leaving me unable to enjoy life as I once did.

But the knowledge that I have a family to protect compelled me to fight back. I'm determined to uncover the identity of Onyx.

Terry wasn't someone I ever suspected, but now I know he's capable of murder. Unfortunately, going to the police seems futile, as I'm certain they wouldn't believe me, and the cafe's patrons would likely cover for Terry. I feel trapped, with an endless list of potential suspects, struggling to find the person behind all of this.

CHAPTER 13

Another day of the James Senior and Layla Smith court case. The courtroom is once again filled with attendees. Among them are Layla's grieving family, Alfie, the Jones Family, Officer Bellis, Luton, Terry, and Oliver.

Two new faces have joined the courtroom proceedings: Terry and Oliver. Officer Bellis stands at the back of the room, accompanied by Luton. Luton, who is currently under suspicion of murder, has somehow been permitted to attend the trial, leaving everyone puzzled.

Alfie appears visibly drained, his worry for his missing brother weighing heavily on him. Many wonder why he has chosen to be present at the trial as they have heard rumours of his brother missing. he is dealing with such significant personal concerns. But still decided to be at court.

The courtroom comes to life as Mister Foster and Mrs Mitchell, the legal representatives, enter, followed by James Senior, who is now dressed in a complete outfit that was bought by Layla. He wears a bright orange jumper and black trousers, a stark contrast to the sombre atmosphere. Locking eyes with his son, James Junior, he offers a smile, to which Junior responds with an awkward one.

The anticipation in the courtroom is palpable as everyone hopes that this might be the final day of the trial, although the ultimate decision rests with the judge.

The first witness chosen by Layla's legal team to take the stand is Officer Bellis, a pivotal figure in the case.

"Your Honour, we would like to call Officer Bellis to the witness stand," announces Mitchell.

This is their opportunity to present all the police evidence and information, shedding light on the truth for the jury.

"Thank you for your time, Mister Bellis. As I understand it, you are the lead officer in the James Senior case, correct?"

"That's correct, ma'am," Officer Bellis affirms.

"What findings have you made since becoming involved in this case?"

"We have accumulated a substantial amount of evidence implicating Mister. Jones on the night in question. Notably, we have identified Mister Jones's DNA on Layla Smith's body."

"Could you elaborate on this evidence?"

"Certainly, We discovered marks on Laylas neck consistent with strangulation, which we attribute to Mister Jones. Additionally, we possess CCTV footage depicting him leaving the pub that night, and ultimately returning home, where he promptly contacted the police."

"Objection, Your Honour! This line of questioning invites speculation, as the witness cannot definitively determine the identity of the perpetrator of the strangulation," Foster interjects with a strenuous objection.

"Mister. Bellis did mention the presence of DNA, Your Honour," the opposing attorney counters. The judge overrules the objection, permitting the continuation of Mister. Bellis's testimony.

"So, Mister. Jones killed her, got in the car, and went to plant the body somewhere."

"Objection!"

"I'll rephrase my question: what evidence did the police have of Mister. Jones when going on the drive?" Mitchell asks.

"We are unsure of where he drove. But the body was found left in a forest near a homeless shelter. The evidence shows that Mister. Jones, when leaving the pub, put on black gloves to try to cover his DNA. We believe the glove had a slight rip caused from his long nails. which is how the evidence has occurred." Officer Bellis says with confidence.

"This helped us find his DNA on her skin."

"So, in your opinion, Mister Bellis, do you believe he killed Layla?" Mitchell asks.

"I do."

"No further questions, your honour."

Once again Mitchell had done a great job of showing evidence of James Senior being the killer that night.

Next, it was Foster's turn. It would be very hard to follow up after what the jury just heard, but he knew he had to distract the jury and change the direction this was going in.

"Nice to meet you, Mister Bellis. I believe you said you don't know where Mister. Jones drove."

"That would be correct, sir." Bellis keeping his confident demeanour.

"So how could you possibly know he drove to this forest?" Foster asks.

"We have multiple CCTV cameras. When Mister Jones' vehicle was spotted multiple times, we just don't have the footage of the forest."

"Oh okay, so the one CCTV camera that actually matters does not exist?" Foster begins to up the pressure.

"Oh yes, but-"

"There's no buts, Mister Bellis. You have no evidence of my client with this dead body. But she has his DNA on him, which could've been his DNA from that night, before that incident. Did you know anything about their relationship?" Foster probed.

"No, of course not, but these were strangling marks."

"They were both passionate, Mister Bellis. These marks could be from consensual activities."

"Your Honour, objection-beyond the question and no evidence of this." Mitchell shouts.

Foster steps in,

Foster steps in,

"Actually, Your Honour, if you go to section fifty-six at the very back, you can see the affectionate, sexual texts from Layla that night." He proceeded to show the texts, which displayed the flirty messages that were sent.

"Sustained."

James Senior looked towards his lawyer with a furious look. Showing his private conversations between him and Layla without his consent.

"Did anyone see him with this body?"

"No, sir." Bellis confirms.

"Could it be possible someone else had the body?" Foster questions.

"Well, there could be-"

Foster interrupts,

"It's just a yes or no, Mister Bellis."

"Yes."

"Exactly. No further questions, your Honour."

It's coming very close to the decision being made, wether James Senior is guilty or not guilty.

The teams were offered another person to bring in on the witness stand. Mitchell decided not to call anyone else to the stand. But Foster has decided take the offer.

"I'd like to call James Junior. to the stand, your Honour." The shock in the courtroom when he announced it. No one knows if he is going to stick up for his father or not. Maybe Junior doesn't even know himself. He begins to walk towards the witness stand and glances at his father. James Senior gives him a little nod.

Junior turns his head away. He's going to be questioned first by Foster.

"Mister Jones, what's your relation to my client?"

"He's my dad."

"Can you tell me about your past with your dad?"

"Sure, we used to be really close and always have meals as a family. He and I would watch football together. He'd always help me with work and give me lifts," The emotion was showing on Juniors face immediately.

"But once he left my mother, we drifted apart a little bit. We still try to see each other every few weeks."

"You were with him that night in the pub, weren't you?" Foster asks.

"Yes, I was."

"Did your dad come across angry or give any signs that night he'd want to hurt Layla?"

"No, he was happy to be watching football with me." He turns to the Jury hoping they have sympathy towards him.

"We had a great night together. We always did."

"Did you ever see him with Layla" Foster asks.

"Yes, I'd always go to their house for the first few hours before we go out. She was lovely. They were lovely together." Junior shares his first smile on the stand.

"Did you ever see him lay a hand on Ms Smith in any harmful way?"

"No, I did not."

"Do you believe your father is capable of this?" Foster continues to ask brutal questions that Junior was compared for.

"Well, after seeing the news, I've got to be honest, I wasn't too sure. But the man I know, the father who brought me up, he is no killer."

"Thank you, Mister. Jones. No further questions, your Honour." Foster walks off.

James Junior came across as an honest man who was hurt, a man who loves his father. But Mitchell knows how mentally vulnerable Junior could be right now with everything he has had to deal with. So, she plans to put the pressure on him.

This is crucial for the case as it's the last person who will be speaking on the witness stand.

James Senior still refuses to go on the witness stand, until his lawyer comes back and whispers in his ear,

"Our best chance is you going on the stand, James. They need to connect with you. Show the jury you're not a monster."

James Senior is certainly thinking about doing it, as it could be his last hope.

Mitchell was ready to put the pressure on Junior and get the answers of the night out.

"You say your father was happy that night out, Mister. Jones?" Mitchell questions.

"Yes, he's always happy with me." Junior looks towards his father and smiles.

"Did he not mention anything negative that night, nothing he's struggling to deal with?"

"No, I don't think so." Junior looks confused.

"Your father was still in love with your mother, wasn't he, Mister Jones?"

"Objection, your Honour, leading." Foster shouts.

"Overruled," the judge responds instantly.

"If we look at the screen here, that we put in evidence, your father seems to be stumbling out of the pub. Mumbling to himself. Looking angry. Would you agree, Mister Jones?"

"Erm, yeah, I guess so."

"If he was happy, in your opinion, why is he getting himself in that state, why is he mumbling to himself? Red-faced. Does he look happy?"

"No." The gasp from the courtroom is deafening from Juniors response.

Mitchell stands tall and proud as she walks back to her table. She seems very confident the way the trial has gone for her. Foster is also still confident that they can win. But he is in need of his last trick up his sleeve. It could be all down to James Senior. if he's willing to testify.

Foster asks the judge for five minutes where he can talk to his client. The judge allows it.

"It's time, James. You've got to do it. For your future." Foster gets passionate.

"I'll do it." He agrees, even though they're both still slightly confident they will win the trial. They believe this will be what tops it all off.

They return to court, and everyone looks confused as they believed there were no more people being called to testify. But they were wrong.

"Your Honour, we'd like to call another witness to the stand."

Mitchell stands up from her chair.

"They can't do this. They've used all their witnesses. They've already had an extra one over us, your Honour."

They go up to the judge where they're battling it out on the decision.

But Mitchell then hears him say who he wants on the witness stand. As soon as she heard it was James Senior, she was happy to allow it. The judge sees both sides are happy, so the judge allows him to testify.

"We'd like to call James Senior to the witness stand." The court couldn't believe it.

They have not heard a word from this man the whole time this case has gone on. The anger on their faces becomes apparent. A roar on Layla's family side. They did not want to hear this man speak; they wouldn't believe anything he had to say. It just brings more anger and rage out.

It all finally settles down, until Alfie raises his voice.

"You've ruined our lives; I hope you rot in hell. I'd kill you; you hear me. I could kill you. I've lost my brother. For what? For you! Dirty murderer!" The police need to calm him down and take him out of the room. The judge orders everyone to be quiet and be seated. He realises the room is getting out of control, so he takes another five minute break.

James Senior decided to stay seated on the witness stand the whole time, watching it all unfold. During these five minutes, James Junior locks eyes with Oliver.

"What are you doing here?" Junior asks aggressively.

Oliver realises he's talking to him.

"I'm interested in what's happening." Oliver retorted.

"Interested in what's going to happen? This is my life. This isn't a TV show. You want drama, do you? I'll give you drama,"

He spits towards Oliver but misses.

"Okay Junior, I'm going to sit over there now," Oliver walks away.

Junior feels hurt by him being here. He opened up and told him everything. But it all seems like it's all just entertainment for Oliver. He felt betrayed.

Was his therapist just getting enjoyment out of the story rather than helping him?

The police kick some people out. Trying to calm the chaos that was happening.

Luton was another who was trying to break through the police to get to James Senior, which wasn't the best idea for him as he could be in this situation himself for murder.

The police eventually calm everyone down. Both Luton and Alfie are eventually allowed back in the room.

It's finally time to question James Senior. and find out what he's been thinking this whole time about his partner being dead and him being the number one suspect.

"So, Mister Jones-"

"Please call me James." He answers in kind tone.

"Okay, James. My first question to you is: how are you feeling?"

James pauses and looks distraught. So much emotion going on.

He composes himself and begins to speak.

"I'm... hurt. You know. I love Layla; I can't accept she's gone. This is a woman I was going to marry. I feel pain, hurt. I feel like everyone in the world believes I could kill her. This is ridiculous." His voice begins to crack up from his emotions.

"How did you find out she was dead?" Fosters brutally asks.

"When the police told me. I thought she was on a night out. She doesn't go out regularly. She loves to stay in, where we would have movie nights. She never stays out late. I knew something was wrong. I called the police about her missing." James was fighting back the tears.

"That must have been hard for you. In your opinion, is there anyone who has a reason to do this?" Foster questioned.

"I know her friends were jealous of what we had. They always treated her awfully because of the love she had towards me."

Someone from the back of the courtroom screams, "Bullshit!"

The police must take another person out of the room.

James Senior doesn't seem phased.

He's making eye contact with the jury and making them feel the pain he has had to go through during this whole process. Thoughts running through his mind. Will his plan pay off, and will the jury decide on "not guilty."

CHAPTER 14

An emotional day for everyone involved, with the town of Emberglade under the world's watchful gaze, all focused on this trial and seeking justice for Layla Smith. James Senior is still being questioned by Mister Foster, and it's challenging to gauge the jury's reaction; the verdict could swing in either direction.

"So, you believe you're innocent, James?" Foster questions.

James turns to the jury.

"I know I'm innocent. We had a holiday booked for Tenerife in a month's time. I enjoyed experiencing life with her. Why on earth would I take her life?"

"What did you do the night you came home that night?"

"I came home, where she had her favourite TV show on pause. But she wasn't home. I checked the time and was worried because, like I said, she was out, and she's always home early."

"And when you got in your car?"

"I got in my car to search for her; I couldn't stay at home being worried. I couldn't find her anywhere. So I drove back home to see if she came back. Still no sign of her, so that's when I called the police."

This was a mistake by Foster mentioning James driving, as he was allegedly drunk that night.

"Okay, last question, James. Why should people believe you're innocent?"

"I'm sure I can't show everyone how innocent I am. But I hope you all today see I'm just a normal man living his life with his beautiful girlfriend. And she's been taken from me; my life has now been ruined. I want justice for Layla."

James Senior. came across as relatable, a local man who appeared broken. The jury felt his pain. However, Layla's family watched in disgust, firmly believing that James Senior was lying to their faces. They thought he had not only murdered Layla but was also disrespecting the memory of her. Mitchell was up next; she had not expected James Senior to testify, but she was still well-prepared in case he did.

"Hello, Mister. Jones."

"Please, you can call me James too."

"That's fine, Mister Jones. Are these your gloves?"

"No, those aren't my gloves."

"Are you really saying this when you've seen we have CCTV footage of you putting on these gloves?"

"You've got footage of me putting on my gloves, not those gloves. Mine are in great condition, not old and ripped like those."

"That's because you ripped them while strangling her, didn't you?"

"Objection, your honour, hearsay!" Mister. Foster objects.

"Sustained." The judge shouts.

Mitchell maintains her professionalism, despite the objections.

"How do you explain your DNA on her body?"

"Well, it's clearly from the night before... this had already been mentioned. From when we made love."

"Did you ever mark her body when making love?"

"No, of course not. Not intentionally."

"Interesting, could we bring up section fifteen, please?"

Mitchell displays two pictures on the screen: a close-up of Layla's body showing a scratch from the nail of the strangle, and another showing bruises all over her arm.

"Can you explain these, then, Mister. Jones?" she asks with a smirk, shaking her finger as if insinuating that he's lying.

James Senior became emotional.

"Why would you show me these? Clearly, the murderer did this."

"These marks have your DNA on them."

"No, I could never. I've never laid a finger on her."

"Can I tell you what I think has happened? I'm gonna tell you anyway. You've come home on a night out, fed up with your life, trying to drink to feel better, which hasn't worked. You knew what you were gonna do that night, which is why you put the gloves on as soon as you left the pub."

"No, you're wrong, you're horrible. Pinning this on me. Horrible!"

"You walk into your home and you see her there, don't you? This is your chance to get the anger out."

"Objection, your honour, none of this is factual; she could be making all this up."

"Sustained, the Jury will forget the last comments."

Mrs Mitchell felt annoyed but continued her questioning.

"Why didn't you call the police right away?"

"I told you I went out to search for her."

"And where did you drive to?"

"Just all over the town."

"What was you doing driving, under the influence of alcohol?"

"I didn't drink that night, you keep saying this not me. I haven't had alcohol in months"

"You was spotted on CCTV Mister Jones. Stumbling, you expect people to believe this? Cameras also spotted you parking near a hospital. Why would you check a hospital, Mister Jones?"

"I checked absolutely everywhere."

"If we review the time when you left your home, got in the car, and the time at the hospital, it's evident that you arrived at the hospital only ten minutes later, which is the same duration it takes to drive from your house to the hospital. Why did you drive there first?"

"I don't know, I wasn't really thinking about where to check first. I just drove."

"Perhaps guilt drove you to take her to the hospital, attempting to save her life and appear as a hero after strangling her?"

"Objection!"

"Don't worry, your honour, I'm finishing up. With the evidence we've presented, Mister Jones, your DNA on her body, your actions captured on camera, and the marks on her neck caused by a rusty glove, do you believe you're innocent?"

"Yes, I've explained why all this has happened..."

"Just a yes or no, please."

"I want to help explain the situations."

"There's nothing more we need to know. No more questions, your honour."

James Senior wanted to scream at Mitchell, but he knew he couldn't afford to appear as an emotional mess. Instead, he gave a little smirk and shook his finger, insinuating that she was lying.

That was rough for James senior, although Mitchell grilled him on the stand. He still game across as a calm and loving man, who answered all the questions very well.

The judge announces that today's trial will end, and the final day will be for the lawyers to give their closing statements.

Luton was immediately taken away by the police after the court adjourned. But why had he been allowed to attend this trial while being under suspicion of murder? The people of Emberglade thought.

Luton found himself in the police station, brought in from his own home. They believed he could be the mysterious killer of Emberglade. The officers aggressively seated him while he was handcuffed.

"What's this, Luton?" Officer Bellis asked aggressively.

Luton squinted his eyes, pretending he doesn't know what the object was.

"I have no idea what that is?"

"It's a mark of your footprint... care to explain how this was in Janice Jones' room?"

Luton's eyes suddenly became serious, but he was certain he had never entered her house. He didn't even know the woman.

"You've got this mistaken, sir. That can't be mine."

"We have no conclusive evidence that this is your footprint, but people have said you was around the area at the time. And I can see you're wearing the exact same shoes of the footprint."

"These are popular shoes. Everyone in Emberglade wears these."

Officer Bellis closed the door and whispered to Luton.

"Listen, I don't think this was your footprint. Maybe it is... I don't care. I know you hate the Jones family, as we all do. I'm sick of them causing this town trouble every day. I want to pin it on James Junior."

Luton couldn't believe what he was hearing. Why would Officer Bellis share this information with him? Bellis was clearly a corrupt cop whose become frustrated with the Jones family. Luton might even be the Onyx himself, but Bellis was running out of options and wanted an ally closely connected to Layla's family who harboured a deep hatred for the Joneses.

"Wow... well, count me in. I absolutely love the idea. I've had enough of that family. Let's see how they react when both the men in their family face consequences."

"Perfect, just remember, if you ever breathe a word about this, I'll change the plan and make you the scapegoat. It's all or nothing, Luton." Bellis has scary threatening look in his eyes.

"I get it." Luton nervously answers.

Luton understood that Bellis had already made this clear to him, that he has no real choice. If he had refused Bellis would ruin his life. But now, he felt secure knowing he had the support of the police, as long as he could implicate James Junior.

CHAPTER 15

In the dead of night, the feeble illumination of a distant streetlight cast eerie, elongated shadows that stretched ominously across James Junior's bedroom. He sat alone, engrossed in a book, unaware of the approaching turmoil. Suddenly, a flicker of movement outside his window seized his attention. His sister, Shannon, clad in dark attire reminiscent of the enigmatic figure known as Onyx, skulked surreptitiously through the yard. A knot of suspicion coiled in his stomach as he observed her every clandestine move, his curiosity piqued to its limit.

With swift decision, he donned sombre garments himself and embarked on a stealthy pursuit. James Junior trailed his sister through the night-shrouded streets, deftly navigating the obscurity as Shannon led him to a nearby house merely five minutes away. Without a second thought, she slipped inside, and James Junior's heart was pounding.

He positioned himself in the shadows, torn between concern for his sister's safety and the unsettling suspicion that her actions might be intricately tied to the town's recent dark occurrences. The feeble illumination of a distant streetlight cast eerie, elongated shadows that stretched ominously across James Junior's bedroom earlier in the night, a stark contrast to his current predicament.

Time crawled by, each minute an eternity, as James grappled with his uncertainty. At long last, Shannon emerged from the house, sprinting homeward, but it did nothing to assuage his disquiet. Driven by the need to unearth the truth, he waited until she had passed before cautiously approaching the house. Standing at the threshold, heart racing, he raised a trembling hand to knock, but there was no response from within.

A gnawing urgency consumed him, and with trepidation escalating, he tested the doorknob. To his astonishment, it yielded under his touch, the door creaking open ominously. Fear and adrenaline surged as he ventured inside, his mind awash with turbulent thoughts. Could his sister be entangled in something nefarious? What if she was linked to the Onyx?

The muffled hum of a television lured him deeper into the house, his steps hesitant yet resolute. Peering cautiously around a corner, his eyes widened in sheer disbelief as they locked onto a girl seated in the dimly lit living room.

A tangled mixture of confusion and terror washed over her features, and she unleashed a spine-chilling scream that reverberated through the air, "ARGHHHH! Get out, get outttt!"

James Junior's panic surged, and he stuttered out an apology, his heart hammering wildly as he stumbled backward and sprinted from the house. His mind raced, breaths coming in ragged gasps. What had he inadvertently stumbled upon? What dark territory had he unknowingly trespassed into? The weight of the eerie encounter bore down upon him as he hastily made his way home, wrestling with a whirlwind of anxiety, fear, and an unsettling sense of uncertainty. He was left wondering about the enigmatic puzzle he had unwittingly set in motion.

As I arrived back at my house, disbelief coursed through me. Had I really been caught snooping around in someone's house once again? I'd managed to slip away unnoticed at Luton's place, but now I found myself breaking into a stranger's home. Stepping into the dimly lit living room, I came face-to-face with Shannon, who was seated on the sofa.

"Where have you been at this hour?" Shannon's questions pierced the air.

"I just needed a walk to clear my head," I offered as an excuse, my heart still racing.

Shannon's eyes gleamed with a peculiar intensity, as if she had unravelled a perplexing mystery. She was acting decidedly strange.

"Alright, I'm heading to bed," I muttered, attempting to put an end to the conversation.

She briskly passed me on her way to her room and promptly locked the door. I couldn't help but wonder if she believed I was the Onyx. It was a colossal misunderstanding. I approached her door and tried to reason with her.

"Shan, can we talk, please?" I implored.

I waited outside her door for what felt like an eternity, but she remained unresponsive. Resigned, I returned to my room and attempted to get some rest. Little did I know that the night held more unpleasant surprises in store.

A sudden and forceful knocking on my door shattered the late-night silence, jolting the entire household awake. I descended to answer the door, puzzled and annoyed by the intrusion. It was the police yet again, and Officer Bellis's familiar face filled me with exasperation.

"James Junior., you're under arrest for breaking and entering, and suspicion of murder," he declared with grim determination.

This couldn't be happening again. It felt as though the police were determined to make my life a living nightmare. Panic surged within me, my mouth went dry, and sweat drenched my palms. I couldn't fathom how they could possibly accuse me of murder. Why on earth would I harm the people my father held dear? They were my family too. This is all too much for me.

I was forcibly taken to the police station, my sleep-deprived mind struggling to comprehend the swift turn of events. There was no evidence of my entry into the house—I had kept my hood up, and there were no security cameras in the vicinity.

Shannon had also entered the house. How had she escaped suspicion? I knew the police would come down hard on me, and I resolved to stay resolute and fight back. There was no way I would let them wrongfully charge me for a mistaken entry and a murder I had not committed.

CHAPTER 16

Back in the police station, the cold metal chair beneath me feels like a merciless reminder of my recurring nightmare. Accused of murdering my own family, especially Aunt Janice whom I loved dearly, I struggle to fathom why someone is relentlessly framing me. Gazing at the drab, lifeless wall, I brace myself for what promises to be the most harrowing interrogation of my life. I can't believe I foolishly followed my sister that fateful night, determined to unveil the Onyx, even if it means exposing her. I can't risk the safety of the rest of my family, but it seems that nobody in this town believes in my innocence.

Officer Bellis strides into the room, his face etched with aggression and seriousness, ready to channel the weight of this complex case onto my shoulders. He slams a file onto the table and follows it up with a clenched fist pounding against the surface. Leaning menacingly over me, he fixes me with a chilling gaze.

"It's quite satisfying to have the killer right here," he sneers.

I can't comprehend how they've pinned me as the murderer. I demand,

"Are you out of your mind? Where's your evidence?"

Officer Bellis's anger escalates, and he delivers a stinging slap across my face.

"Things are about to get a whole lot worse for you, kid, unless you start talking right now!" he hisses.

Despite the pain, I muster a defiant laugh. He can't just assault people because he's a cop.

"Enjoy that? I'll see to it that you lose your badge for this," I retort.

"Listen, do you honestly believe anyone here will listen to a whining little murderer like you instead of me?" Officer Bellis taunts, a smug grin etching onto his face.

He reaches into his bag of evidence, producing a footprint I've never seen before. It couldn't possibly match mine. With force, he slams it onto the floor and orders me to place my foot over it. My heart sinks as I realise it's a perfect match. The walls seem to close in around me, and the dread of impending doom tightens its grip.

In the midst of the conversation, Officer Bellis continued his talk and, with a sarcastic tone, quipped,

"Oh, what a perfect fit." The atmosphere hung with tension as his words settled in the air.

I stood there, aghast at the damning evidence before me. My foot slid neatly into the incriminating print, and shock rendered me speechless.

"We're aware you've broken into two houses, James. I'm sure there are more incidents where you were more lucky... Have you taken innocent lives, James?" Bellis taunted.

I couldn't muster a response, but tears welled up in my eyes. Bellis relished my anguish, his laughter an unsettling echo in the room. I was utterly alone, trapped with an officer who showed no regard for rules, willing to use his crowbar to extract the answers he wanted. He exited the room, leaving me trembling in his wake.

Another officer took his place, and I desperately tried to recount the injustice Bellis had subjected me to. However, my explanations fell on deaf ears, met with scepticism or indifference. The thought crossed my mind: what if my father fell victim to this sinister manipulation as well? If they could accuse me of murder while I was innocent, what was to stop them from doing the same to him?

Left overnight in the cell, Bellis's nefarious plan unfolded precisely as he had intended. When the call came in, reporting that I had broken into a girl's house, he saw it as a stroke of luck, a jackpot.

Luton feigned satisfaction with their "successful plan," but as soon as the call ended with Bellis , he hurled the phone to the ground in frustration. His attempt to pin the blame on Alfie had failed, but he wasn't ready to give up. He possessed another untraceable phone, and he was reverting to his original plan, the one he had initiated before Bellis had come knocking on his door with threats. With newfound determination, he picked up the phone and sent a chilling text to Alfie:

"I have your brother... If you want him back, confess to the Emberglade murders."

Had Luton indeed kidnapped Alfie's brother, or was he bluffing to ensnare Alfie and ensure his imprisonment?

Alfie's nights had transformed from commanding the mob to wandering the desolate streets of Emberglade, consumed by the relentless search for his missing brother. His eyes bore the painful marks of sleepless nights, sporting fiery red rings that testified to his unyielding determination. Day after day, he revisited the same locations, fervently hoping for a miraculous reunion that never came. He refused to surrender to despair.

Amid his relentless pursuit, Alfie's phone buzzed with a message from an unfamiliar number. His heart raced as he read the words, and instinctively, he scanned his surroundings, half-expecting the sender to be lurking nearby.

"Come out and speak to me in person, you coward!" Alfie bellowed into the empty streets, but there was no response, no one in sight.

Overwhelmed, he collapsed into a sea of tears. His last remaining family member had been ripped away from him, leaving Alfie to grapple with the daunting task of caring for his vulnerable brother alone. The text hinted at a sinister ultimatum, forcing Alfie to consider a terrible choice. He contemplated sacrificing his own freedom to protect his brother, who already bore the weight of a debilitating condition.

In Emberglade, trust was a rare commodity, and Alfie had no inkling of the person behind this cruel message. Alfie sent a concise reply,

"Let's meet up, and we'll discuss the deal."

Frustration and anger boiled within him as he unleashed a primal scream into the uncaring night. He had no other option. He prayed the sender would agree to the meeting and bring his brother. Only then could he reclaim his sibling and unveil the identity of the kidnapper.

As Alfie headed home, he navigated the labyrinth of the mob. Terry, one of its members, spotted him and called him over, oblivious to Alfie's anguish and the cryptic message that hung over him like a shroud.

"Alfie, where have you been? We miss you," Terry pleaded, hoping Alfie would rejoin their ranks.

"Not now, Terry, alright?" Alfie responded curtly.

Terry was bewildered by Alfie's sudden withdrawal from their cause.

"What's wrong? You're not siding with the Jones family now, are you?" Terry prodded.

"Never mention that again," Alfie snapped, grabbing Terry by the neck before quickly releasing him, aware that drawing attention would be unwise

"That man deceived me. I would never be friends with a killer." Alfie shouted.

"Just wondering why you're not protesting with us anymore, Alfie," Terry pressed, seeking clarity.

Alfie offered a brief apology and walked away, refusing to divulge the torment he was enduring. He had no desire for sympathy, knowing that the mob wouldn't be able to aid him in finding his brother.

Rumours of James Junior's arrest had spread like wildfire through the mob, sparking both jubilation and increased fervour among its members. They were eager to rid their town of the Jones family, who had become the pariahs of Emberglade, reviled not only locally but also globally.

News outlets had hit record-high viewership whenever discussing the case, and social media was ablaze with opinions and judgments. Some valiantly defended the Jones family, but they were a minority against the overwhelming chorus demanding the entire family's incarceration, even the innocent women who had committed no wrongdoing.

Terry had ascended to the role of mob leader, anointing himself as the town's self-proclaimed hero. He couldn't help but harbour regrets about his failed attempt to poison James Senior. with glass in his food, wishing he had succeeded in ending the family's reign of turmoil. Now, he was determined to continue making their lives unbearable. Strangely, Terry had maintained a facade of friendliness towards James Junior. Despite his natural shyness, if they were to cross paths now, his demeanour would likely be starkly different.

As night descended, the mob reluctantly dispersed, unable to achieve their goal of driving the Jones family out of town. The police had erected barricades around the family's home to ensure their safety. Everyone was bracing themselves for the impending climax of the trial—the closing statements in James Senior's case.

CHAPTER 17

Alfie remained gripped by terror as he anxiously awaited a response from the mysterious kidnapper. Hours passed, each minute feeling like an eternity. Unable to bear the agony of uncertainty, he eventually returned home and, consumed by rage and frustration, unleashed a torrent of destruction upon his surroundings. The sound of his screams reverberated through the walls, echoing onto the streets outside.

Suddenly, his phone emitted a piercing beep, signalling a text message from the enigmatic kidnapper. It read,

"You want to meet me, you know what to do."

Alfie's anger surged anew. The kidnapper refused to relent, demanding that Alfie step forward as the Onyx—a choice that would obliterate his reputation, lock him away for life, and sever any chance of reuniting with his beloved brother. This was an unthinkable option; Alfie had to devise a plan.

Meanwhile, James Junior grappled with his own struggles as the relentless cases in Emberglade exacted an unbearable toll on the town's reputation. Businesses shuttered, and fear had immobilised the populace, rendering them prisoners in their own homes amid the shadow of these alleged murderers.

Officer Bellis traversed the room where Junior was confined for the night. He noticed Junior gazing blankly at the ceiling, absentmindedly scratching the floor. Junior's mind raced with thoughts of his father facing the same dire predicament. Their sparse finances left them unable to afford bail, ensnaring them in the prison's clutches until they were cleared of the Emberglade murderer label. Bellis approached, delivering a meagre meal of a single piece of bread and an apple. It was enough sustenance to endure the day.

As Junior reached for the food, Bellis leaned in and whispered,

"You and your father are going to be gone for a long time." He sought a reaction, but James met his gaze with unwavering resolve.

"You'll regret this," he retorted coldly.

"Once the real killer is found, you'll lose your job, and I'll relish every moment when they strip that badge from you."

With that, Bellis callously tossed Junior's food onto the filthy floor and walked away.

Amid the storm of accusations, Junior held tightly to the knowledge of his innocence, maintaining a quiet confidence that the truth would eventually come to light. Despite his conviction, Bellis, along with the entire Emberglade community and the online world, vehemently disagreed.

Emberglade Prison was renowned for its harsh and unforgiving environment, notorious as one of the toughest correctional facilities in the United Kingdom. It primarily housed individuals convicted of the gravest crimes, including murder and rape. Unlike some other prisons with organised gangs, this institution employed a different strategy— confining inmates to solitary cells for most of the day.

Their rare moments of respite occurred only during mealtimes or for a brief breath of fresh air. Friendships were a rarity, and camaraderie was absent, as each inmate adopted a dog-eat-dog mentality.

The seclusion, the endless monotony, and the deprivation of human interaction took a heavy toll on the prisoners' mental well-being. Consequently, when they did encounter another human being, it was often seen as an opportunity to experience something— anything—again. This could lead to confrontations, verbal assaults, or even acts of violence.

James Senior had already endured his share of harsh experiences within this unforgiving prison. Word spread like wildfire, especially in a place like Emberglade Prison, where many inmates hailed from the local community and could instantly recognise familiar faces. One day, an inmate ordered James Senior to remove his shirt, a demand James staunchly refused.

The man had no intention of repeating himself and granted James. a final chance to comply, but he remained steadfast in his refusal. In response, the towering man seized James by the back of the head and brutally slammed his face against the unyielding kitchen counter.

James, well aware that he couldn't afford to engage in any fights while facing trial, endured the assault without retaliation.

He crumpled to the cold floor, the man callously hurled the remainder of his food at him and delivered a punishing kick to his stomach, followed by a brutal blow to his already battered face. Finally, the intervention of prison authorities put an end to the savage ordeal. James was left on the floor, marked by his own blood, his vision blurred and head throbbing. This cruel experience served as his stark wake-up call to the grim life that awaited him.

James was swiftly taken to the prison doctor, relieved to find that his face had escaped any visible cuts or bruises that might be used against him in the courtroom. The prison doctor's job was a gruelling one, with violence being a daily occurrence in Emberglade Prison. Many doctors had come and gone, unable to withstand the constant stress and danger of their environment.

These professionals were not renowned for their social skills, and the inmates' disdain for them ran deep. But Doctor Jenkins saw something different in James Senior. Despite the fresh signs of a brutal attack, he remained polite and showed kindness to the doctor, a stark contrast to the hostility the doctor typically encountered.

She knew that James had little chance of survival in this perilous place. The inmates viewed "likeable" individuals as prime targets, considering them the most disliked.

"You should avoid talking to these people in here, you know," Doctor Jenkins cautioned James.

He responded with a wry smile, "I'll be fine. It's par for the course. I'm not exactly on vacation, am I?" Doctor Jenkins couldn't help but smirk at his response.

"Just steer clear of the fights. You won't make it here otherwise." Her advice, while well-intentioned, struck James as a blow to his pride.

He couldn't help but feel weak and incapable of defending himself. But he knew that retaliating was not an option. With the clock ticking, the identity of the Emberglade killer remained shrouded in mystery.

James Junior found himself incarcerated in the same prison as his father but remained separated by their release times, preventing them from reuniting. However, James Junior's time in prison was short-lived, as someone had paid his bail.

The news left Junior incredulous. No one in his circle had the financial means to pay for his release, and he couldn't believe it when the officer informed him. The satisfaction he gleaned from Bellis's bewildered expression was immeasurable. The corrupt cop would soon face karma for his actions. He thought.

There were few things worse than a crooked police officer.

"You can leave now, Mister Jones," he was told, and the joy was nearly impossible to contain as he was escorted out of the prison.

The confinement had been agonising, and the prospect of reuniting with his family filled him with hope.

Curiosity gnawed at him as he wondered who had paid his bail. As the police officer opened the door to release him, he found himself face to face with a towering figure, his curiosity piqued.

The unexpected saviour was Oliver, his therapist. Junior couldn't fathom why Oliver had bailed him out, especially considering their strained parting. Gratitude welled up within him, yet confusion lingered. Despite their past differences, he warmly embraced Oliver with a handshake and a hug as they exited the prison. The rush of fresh air against his skin felt like a rejuvenating wave, as though he had been imprisoned for years rather than days.

"Thank you so much for getting me out of there, Oliver. I owe you," Junior expressed his deep gratitude.

Oliver's response was simple and heartfelt,

"Don't worry about it. I was genuinely concerned about your well-being."

Junior, while immensely grateful, couldn't help but inquire further,

"I don't mean to sound ungrateful, but why did you bail me out? I understand you were worried, but we barely know each other."

A sly smirk tugged at Oliver's lips as he responded,

"I know you better than you might think, Junior."

It was a stark reminder that Junior had seldom opened up to anyone about his life and the complex dynamics within his family, except during his sessions with Oliver.

"Be cautious, Junior," Oliver continued, his tone turning more serious.

"This town harbours some truly malevolent individuals. Trust no one. Go home safely to your family."

Junior nodded, his heart filled with a single desire—to return home. Oliver's unexpected act of kindness had given him a second chance, and he would forever be in his debt. As he made his way home, he couldn't help but wonder if his family would believe in his innocence as they had initially believed in his father's guilt.

CHAPTER 18

Arriving at my home, I bid farewell to Oliver, a mix of gratitude and anxiety coursing through me. The prospect of entering my own house felt strangely unfamiliar and worrisome.

None of my family had visited me during my time in prison, but I held no grudge against them. After all, I stood accused of a heinous crime, and now I was returning to live under the same roof as them.

It was 7:00 PM, and I could only guess what my family might be doing inside. Perhaps they were gathered in the living room watching TV together, or each was locked away in their own rooms, contending with their own emotions.

The weight of their lives falling apart mirrored my own. My dreams of opening a café or restaurant had been shattered, and the entire town seemed to harbour a collective desire for my downfall.

Steeling myself, I opened the back door, which led me into the kitchen. Taking a deep breath, I pushed open the door that separated the kitchen from the living room. There they were—my mother and two sisters seated on the sofa.

Their heads turned in unison as they heard the door slam and witnessed my entrance. Their expressions were an enigma, a complex mix of emotions—perhaps happiness, fear, anger, or a tangled amalgamation of all three. I couldn't decipher their true feelings.

My mother stood up, her footsteps heavy with the burden of emotions she carried. She approached me, her hand connecting with my cheek in a sharp slap. It stung, but I knew I deserved it. I stood there, bearing the weight of her anger and disappointment.

Then, as if a dam had burst, my mother began to cry, burying her face in my shoulder. In that moment, her tears revealed her enduring love for me, mingled with profound worry about what the future held for our family.

My sisters approached as a united front, their emotions running high and their voices filled with tension.

"Did you do it, Junior? I swear to God, if you did, then get out of our house," Shannon struggled to contain her frustration, her words biting with accusation.

"Of course I didn't do it! I'm being framed. You've got some nerve to accuse me," I snapped back, regretting my outburst in front of the entire family.

"Excuse me, what are you trying to say, huh?" Shannon squared up to me, but Selena intervened, attempting to hold her back.

"He's our brother, Shannon. Please, stop it. I can't take it," Selena pleaded, struggling to restrain her fiery sister.

"Maybe you were the one involved in all this, framing me, wanting me arrested or dead," I said, my voice trembling.

"Are you for real? You know what, James? Maybe you're right, because I'd love to murder you right now," Shannon screamed, her anger flaring.

"Yeah, I bet you do. Some sister you are. Where did you sneak off to that night? I followed you. Come on, tell me the truth. Did you set me up?" I challenged, my accusations hanging heavy in the air.

"Stop it, stop it now!" My mum's voice rose in distress as she watched her family teetering on the brink of conflict.

"Take it to your room, Mum," I urged, my patience wearing thin.

My mum had no other choice but to leave the room; the stress was too much for her.. She couldn't bear to leave Selena caught between the two of us, but she had to get away from the escalating tension.

"Set you up? Don't make me laugh," Shannon retorted, her voice dripping with sarcasm.

"Yeah, I bet you did. Wouldn't surprise me if you set up Dad too!" I was accused.

In a fit of rage, Shannon threw Selena to the floor and lunged at me. Desperate to defuse the situation, I closed the door on her and bolted out of the house. I couldn't even find solace in my own home anymore.

As I sprinted away, the thought lingered: Could Shannon have been the Onyx all along?

Junior. had no choice but to spend the night in a hotel, but sleep eluded him as paranoia gnawed at his thoughts. He racked his brain for a way to escape the impending jail time for a crime he didn't commit.

Meanwhile, Alfie was on a mission not just to find his brother but also to track down the mysterious caller and seek vengeance.

Alfie recalled a guy he used to train with in boxing, who had coding skills and could hack into phones or trace them. He reached out to him and explained the dire situation. The guy was eager to help. After two days of relentless effort, he couldn't hack into the caller's phone but managed to pinpoint a potential location.

Alfie wasted no time. He armed himself for protection and headed toward the given location, his mind racing with worry for his brother, hoping he was still alive, though he had already endured so much in life.

Alfie's arrival at the specified location was accompanied by a thundering heartbeat and clammy palms, shrouded in an aura of uncertainty. He found himself in a desolate, decrepit warehouse, situated on the outskirts of town. The dimly lit space bore an eerie silence that hung heavy in the air.

Dust particles danced lazily in the feeble light streaming through shattered windows, casting disconcerting shadows. In this unsettling setting, Alfie was about to confront the enigmatic kidnapper.

With a gun tucked into the back of his jeans, Alfie braced himself, fully aware that he might have to resort to using it. Despite the tension gripping him, he knew he had to maintain his composure.

Pushing open the creaking, rust-covered door, the sound reverberated throughout the warehouse, amplifying the eerie atmosphere. Inside, darkness enveloped him, and he strained to make out anything in the murky expanse.

Anxious that someone may be there. He called out, demanding the kidnapper to reveal themselves. Silence met his words, but suddenly, the flickering of a dim light in the corner of his eye caught his attention.

Unbeknownst to Alfie, his brother lay in that corner, out of his wheelchair, sprawled on the floor. Though still alive, he bore visible bruises from the rough treatment he had endured at the hands of the mysterious kidnapper.

"I'm not here to play games! Show yourself, you coward!" Alfie's voice reverberated through the warehouse.

It was then that he received a response, a voice deliberately altered to conceal the speaker's identity.

The lights flickered intermittently, heightening the tension in the room. Slowly, a figure emerged from the shadows, shrouded in a dark, hooded cloak and concealing their face behind a mask. This was the elusive kidnapper, their true identity hidden behind layers of clothing and a mechanised voice. Was it Luton, orchestrating a plan to frame

Alfie, or could this be the Onyx? It remained impossible to ascertain from their attire and disguised voice. The truth lurked in the shadows, waiting to be unveiled.

"It's a surprise seeing you here, Alfie. What brings you into my home?"

"You know damn well why I'm here, you bastard," Alfie seethed with anger, his hand itching to reach for the gun concealed in his jeans.

"Now, now, let's keep our manners. You do care about your brother, don't you?" The kidnapper nodded towards the henchmen guarding Alfie's brother, who callously kicked the defenceless man.

In a burst of fury, Alfie lunged at the men who had assaulted his brother. He tackled one to the ground, but the other quickly grabbed him, locking him in a choking grip. As Alfie struggled for breath, the man he had taken down rose to his feet and landed a brutal punch to Alfie's ribs.

At that moment, the guard's fingers brushed against something tucked in his jeans—his gun. Without hesitation, he snatched it and hurled it in the direction of the mysterious kidnapper.

"I did attempt to give you a fair warning, Alfie," the kidnapper sneered, indicating the small, ominous cage they had unceremoniously thrown Alfie into. There seemed to be no feasible escape route.

The kidnapper's gaze bore into Alfie as he issued a menacing ultimatum,

"You can clearly see we've upheld our end of the bargain. Now, it's time for you to shoulder the blame for every murder that has plagued Emberglade."

"Go to hell," Alfie retorted, his defiance palpable as he spat towards his captor, resolutely refusing to comply with the kidnapper's demands.

The kidnapper presses the gun to Joel's forehead as Alfie begs him not to shoot. "No please, I'll say I'm the Onyx, just don't do this!"

"Should've been your first answer," the kidnapper replies coldly before pulling the trigger.

Alfie watches in horror as his brother is murdered mere feet away. He shakes the cage violently, screaming and throwing himself against the bars trying to break free, but only causes himself more pain.

Collapsing to his hands and knees, Alfie is overwhelmed with disbelief. The Onyx has just executed his helpless brother right before his eyes.

As Alfie sobs uncontrollably, the Onyx calmly departs the warehouse, locking the door behind them. Alfie realises he's been left trapped there, perhaps to die beside his brother's body.

Rage and anguish churn inside Alfie; he should've done more to protect Joel, he believed.

But it's too late now - the Onyx sadistically ripped away the only family Alfie had left.

Exhausted and defeated, Alfie curls up on the cold floor. He wants to give up, but knows Joel would want him to keep fighting.

Closing his eyes, Alfie makes a silent vow - he will escape this place and avenge his brother, no matter what it takes. The Onyx will regret the day they crossed paths with the two of them.

CHAPTER 19

The town of Emberglade had sunk into the depths of despair. A wave of unsolved murders had plunged the community into fear, and the police were grappling with the relentless hunt for the killer.

The lingering mystery surrounding James Senior's case cast a dark shadow over the town, and each night, unruly mobs led by Terry wreaked havoc in the streets.

Residents lived in perpetual unease, their properties and public spaces defiled, even a once-peaceful park reduced to ashes. The Jones family, too, fell victim to the turmoil, their home's windows shattered in a brazen attack.

Emberglade, had transformed into the most perilous and violent place imaginable.

Amidst this reign of terror, James Junior yearned for a semblance of normalcy and the comforting presence of Oliver. He longed to confide in someone about the madness engulfing their town. However, as he tapped out messages to Oliver, his phone remained hauntingly silent. Oliver had vanished since posting his bail. James couldn't fathom why someone would expend considerable resources to secure his release, only to then vanish into the ether.

Alone in a ramshackle hotel room, James grew increasingly desperate to reunite with his family. He was running low on funds and couldn't afford to spend more nights in such accommodations. If he were to make amends with his estranged family, he'd have to place his trust in Shannon. But Shannon harboured her own suspicions and fears, making it a precarious alliance.

As James switched on the television, his heart plummeted. His own name flashed across the screen, accused of being the harbinger of these gruesome murders. He struggled to comprehend how the blame had been placed squarely upon his shoulders. The stress of the situation threatened to consume him. Desperate for a respite, he decided to venture out into the night, craving the solace of fresh air after being confined to his stifling hotel room for an agonising night.

Leaving the confines of the hotel behind, James embarked on a solitary walk through the desolate streets of Emberglade.

Few cars dared to venture out, as the fear that gripped the town had driven most residents to remain within the safety of their homes. The stroll, however, failed to provide the mental respite he so desperately sought.

As he traversed the familiar path, he couldn't help but cast a glance towards the corner shop, a place forever etched in his memory for the traumatic murder of his aunt. The haunting experience continued to torment his thoughts, and this walk did little to alleviate his distress.

Suddenly, in the distance, James's eyes locked onto a face he recognised. The figure, Luton, seemed to be scanning his surroundings with a sense of unease. Their eyes met, and James detected a hint of fear in Luton's gaze. Perplexed by this reaction, James speculated that perhaps Luton had been influenced by the recent news reports. Before he could decipher more, Luton darted away, leaving James contemplating whether to give chase. He hesitated, mindful that pursuing Luton might cast suspicions upon him, as if he were chasing another potential victim.

Reluctantly, he abandoned the pursuit, choosing instead to head home. However, upon arrival, a shattered window caught his attention, sparking immediate concern. Worried that something had befallen his family, he pushed open the door and entered.

Inside, he found his mother and Selena, though their demeanour was far from what he expected. They sat together, but not at the dinner table where they used to gather as a family. They were perched on the sofa, their eyes wary and guarded. They attempted to find solace in a comedy TV series, attempting to muster a smile, but it was clear that no comedian could banish the weight of their worries.

As James settled into the sofa opposite them, he sensed an unsettling tension in the air, a palpable fear of his presence. He had thought that both his mother and Selena believed in his innocence, but it appeared Shannon had managed to sow seeds of doubt in their minds.

Desperate to bridge the divide, he attempted to initiate a light-hearted conversation, inquiring about their activities. Selena's response, however, came across as pointing,

"Nothing much, just looking after Mum." The undertone seemed to carry a subtle accusation.

The tension in the household was palpable, looming like a dark cloud as they all awaited the impending trial of their father. This pivotal moment would determine whether he was truly innocent or not. But even if the judge were to proclaim him guilty, Junior struggled to place his faith in a justice system that appeared riddled with corruption. They were hell-bent on pinning murders on Junior, tearing his life apart.

As the trial drew near, Junior clung to the hope that if his father could prove his innocence, it might serve as a beacon, guiding them back to a semblance of normalcy, remaining confident that the truth would eventually reveal that he was not a murderer.

Junior's mother's gaze bore into him, a mixture of anxiety and disgust, as she posed a haunting question.

"James, did you do it? I need the truth. This is killing me" she cried

"No, Mum, I didn't. I promise. I'm living in constant fear, and I don't know what to do," Junior replied, his voice quivering with emotion.

Relief washed over Junior as his mother seemed to believe his words. She approached Junior with a warm, reassuring hug.

"I can't bear to lose you too, Junior," she whispered, shattering his heart.

Her words made Junior feel like a failure, a terrible son who had let down the person who meant the most to her.

"Come back home, Junior. You're safe here," his mother implored.

He desperately wanted to say yes, to return to the comfort of their family home. But he couldn't bear the thought of being anywhere near Shannon. So, Junior conjured up an excuse to decline her offer and left.

The journey back to the hotel was a cold and lonely Twenty-minute walk through dimly lit streets, marred by the remnants of the mobs' protests.

Throughout his ordeal, Junior had managed to evade the menacing mob that had been terrorising the town. So he thought. As Junior made his way back to the hotel on that fateful night, it seemed his luck was about to change.

As I made my way home, distant chants echoed through the air. These ominous voices grew more fervent as night fell, knowing that it would attract attention. The chilling realisation that my own town, the place where I'd known everyone my entire life, now resounded with guttural screams and demands for my demise, sent shivers down my spine.

Among the crowd, one man's voice rang out, singling me out,

"Oi, no way! The murderer... he's there!"

My instincts kicked in instantly, and I sprinted away, aware that the mob would pursue me relentlessly if they got close. The mob resembled a horde of possessed zombies, driven by a thirst for my blood.

I veered into a hidden alleyway, nestled between houses where I'd grown up. From the shadows, I watched the frenzied mob rush past, my heart pounding in my chest. After a few nerve-wracking minutes, I cautiously stepped out, thinking I was finally in the clear. But I couldn't have been more wrong.

"Hello, Junior," a familiar voice sent a chill down my spine. I whirled around to find Oliver standing behind me.

I hadn't heard from him since he bailed me out, and his presence initially brought relief. However, something had changed about him – an unsettling intensity in his eyes, as though he aimed to intimidate me.

"Do you have a problem, mate? You never answered my calls, and now you appear out of nowhere," I said, baffled, as I believed we had no unresolved issues.

"Bet you did it, didn't you. You killed them" Oliver accused, his tone accusatory.

"Listen, I had nothing to do with it, okay? Why did you bail me out if you think that?" I retorted.

"Maybe because I wanted you here in town, where everyone wants you dead," he replied, his demeanour cold and distant.

I was taken aback, realising that our relationship ran deeper than I had thought.

"Where is all this coming from? You were just my therapist; you're nobody," I protested.

"No, Junior, I was your dad's best mate when you were younger. He swindled my money, disrespected me and my family, and now, he's a filthy little murderer just like you," Oliver revealed, his eyes gleaming with a vindictive satisfaction that chilled me to the bone.

All along, I had believed that he only knew me through the news, but I had been profoundly mistaken. I had confided in this man, placed my trust in him, only to discover that he relished my suffering, fuelled by his hatred for my father.

"So, are you planning to kill me yourself? Try it!" I challenged, my defensiveness growing as I realised I had to stand my ground.

"I won't need to do that. I'm sure someone else will. Take your pick, Junior," he responded ominously.

As Oliver walked away, his chilling words continued to echo in my mind, a haunting refrain that followed me back to my hotel. The weight of his accusations bore down on me, and I couldn't shake the creeping fear that he might be right. It seemed inevitable that someone in this town would eventually make an attempt on my life. At that moment, I felt like the most reviled man in the world, second only to my father.

This encounter with Oliver was a stark reminder that trust was a rare commodity in this town. It was inhabited by a community of arrogant individuals who believed they held all the answers.

James Junior spent another lonely night in the hotel, hidden from the relentless pursuit of the mob, whose determination to find him showed no signs of waning. His sense of safety had reached an all-time low.

The streets were plagued by violence, lives were being extinguished, and the town's most sensational trial had become the topic of conversation. Visitors were a distant memory; the town was now a grim haven for fearful and enraged residents who struggled to come to terms with the fact that one of their own, a member of their community, might be a murderer—perhaps even the infamous Onyx.

As the sun rose, casting a pale glow on the cramped hotel room's walls and the uncomfortable tiny bed where James Junior had spent another restless night, he realised that a momentous day loomed ahead. It was the day everyone had been eagerly awaiting—the culmination of James Senior's court trial.

CHAPTER 20

A momentous day dawned, poised to shape the lives of many. All eyes were fixed on the impending trial, with the hope that the jury would not succumb to the overwhelming social media vitriol aimed at James Senior. However, the pervasive online hatred was difficult to ignore. Even the lawyers themselves seemed uneasy, aware that the outcome could propel or shatter their careers, given the immense public interest in the case. But perhaps the most pivotal aspect was whether Layla's truth would prevail, ensuring that the right person faced justice.

The courtroom was brimming with familiar faces, many of them wearing expressions that betrayed their anticipation, as they expected James Senior to receive a life sentence.

Terry was accompanied by some friends from the mob, while Oliver and Luton stood alone. Selena and Shannon sat side by side, but their mother couldn't bear to witness the proceedings and chose to stay home. At the front, James Junior anxiously bit his fingernails, desperately trying to suppress thoughts of the worst outcome. Officer Bellis was on duty once again, though there was no sign of Alfie.

Then, the moment arrived as James Senior entered the room, dressed in a suit.

A barrage of hateful words erupted as soon as he came into view, and a nervous smirk played on his lips in response to the palpable loathing directed his way. The judge promptly called for order, instructing everyone to be seated.

It was now time for the lawyers to deliver their closing statements to the jury.

The fate of the case rested in the hands of the lawyers, who had just ten minutes to summarise the entire proceedings, present their arguments to the jury, and explain why James Senior was either guilty or not guilty.

First to address the jury was Layla's lawyer, Mrs Mitchell. She positioned a large whiteboard behind her, adorned with pictures depicting the bruises, a timestamped image of James leaving the pub, and select quotations from witnesses.

Mitchell commenced her closing statement with a warm tone, acknowledging the fatigue that had likely settled upon the jury after enduring the trial. A ripple of chuckles passed through the jurors in response to her comment.

"Good evening, ladies and gentlemen of the jury. I want to express my gratitude for your unwavering dedication throughout this trial. I'm certain you've sacrificed as many hours of sleep as I have," she began, her eyes scanning the faces of the jurors.

"Today is the day where you can deliver justice for Layla Smith," she continued, gesturing towards the heavens, invoking the concept of a higher moral order.

"The man sat before you had taken the stand himself, looked you in the eyes, and spun lies. Do not be deceived by this man. He may attempt to present himself as a composed, amiable individual, but make no mistake – he is not. James Jones Senior is a man who is frail, damaged, and deeply broken. A man who derives pleasure from inflicting harm upon women."

Mitchell's finger pointed assertively at the bruised image of Layla.

"Does this bruise resemble a mere stumble to you? Of course not. It is a bruise inflicted through the physical abuse James Jones subjected Layla Smith to. Whenever he returned home from work or a night out, violence would follow."

She redirected their attention to the picture of him leaving the pub.

"Which brings us to the night in question, as he stumbled out of the pub. He claims he had not consumed much alcohol, but the CCTV footage suggests otherwise. He was seen donning gloves. Why would someone suddenly put on gloves if not to obscure their fingerprints?" Agreement seemed to resonate among the jurors.

"James entered the house, and the mere sight of Layla triggered him. He lunged towards her, channelling every ounce of his strength to slam her to the ground. Punching, kicking – you name it, he did it. Until he wrapped his hands around her throat, squeezing the life out of her.

These are the grim facts that transpired at the crime scene within James Jones's residence."

Mitchell paced back to the whiteboard, highlighting the incriminating witness statements.

"CCTV footage conclusively identifies him as the perpetrator," she emphasised.

"The black gloves have been incontrovertibly linked to James Jones's attire. The fingerprints were linked to James and he was witnessed fleeing his home shortly after the time of the victim's death. Furthermore, evidence suggests he habitually abused Layla, isolating her from family and friends." Each statement was carefully displayed on the board, strengthening her argument.

"This is the undeniable evidence that you've been presented with throughout this trial," Mitchell declared with conviction.

"I'm certain that Mister Foster will weave a compelling narrative, a believable but fabricated story, in an attempt to paint James as innocent. However, ladies and gentlemen of the jury, actions speak louder than words.

No explanation can justify the actions captured by CCTV, confirmed by DNA, and substantiated by the evidence before you. No words can absolve James of his guilt because he is not innocent. I implore you not to be swayed by his deceit. Your verdict in this trial should unequivocally declare James Jones Senior as guilty."

The jury's expressions remained inscrutable, but it appeared as though they were nodding in agreement with the arguments presented.

The rest of the courtroom, except for the Jones family, was awash with emotion, proud of the compelling closing statement that brought them one step closer to seeing justice served and the accused behind bars.

Layla's family wept tears of both gratitude and sorrow, feeling as though they were witnessing a champion fighting for their daughter's life. Their father's testimony on the witness stand had been a harrowing experience, and they had done everything they could to seek justice for Layla. In contrast, the Jones family appeared fatigued and strained, unable to display any emotion.

As the judge prepared to call upon Mister Foster to present his closing statement, a sudden outbreak of commotion disrupted the proceedings, with Luton engaged in an altercation with Officer Bellis. The unprofessional exchange prompted another officer to intervene and instruct Officer Bellis to leave, but he refused, asserting his seniority,

"I'm your boss; don't you dare speak to me that way." Bellis demanded.

"The courtroom was baffled by the unprofessionalism of Officer Bellis, causing disruption during the tense trial."

After the courtroom was finally restored to order, the judge signalled for Foster to begin his closing statement.

The room fell into complete silence, and all eyes were fixed on James Senior. Could Foster convince the jury of James's innocence? this was their last chance, and the gravity of the moment hung heavily in the air as James began his closing statement.

CHAPTER 21

Foster approached the jury, a familiar act for him, but today, nerves pulsed beneath his practised exterior. He arranged his whiteboard, displaying a happy picture of James and Layla, with the word "killer" crossed out and followed by a question mark, alongside the word "DNA."

"Good evening, ladies and gentlemen of the jury. I empathise with the daunting task before you today. You hold not only Mister Jones's life in your hands but also Layla's and her family's quest for closure. They seek peace through the conviction of the true culprit. To find true peace, we need to capture the correct murderer. The man before you is not that killer," Mister. Foster began, his voice resolute as he walked toward the board

He retrieved the picture of James and Layla, blissfully captured during a happier time.

"They were an undeniably happy couple, as numerous witnesses have attested, testifying to their profound love. My question to you is simple – why? Why would he end her life? What possible motive could he have, other than to lose the love of his life?"

Shannon, sitting in the crowd, couldn't help but let out a sceptical chuckle, unconvinced by Foster's words about her father.

"Mrs Mitchell has referenced the presence of my client's DNA on Layla's body. But consider this: James and Layla spent the night together, as they often did. They lived together, sharing every moment of their lives. What you should be searching for are the individuals with motives. James Jones loved and cared for this women," Foster continued, his confidence mounting with each word.

"Layla's family deserves justice, the right man to be held accountable. It falls on your shoulders, esteemed members of the jury. They have no substantial evidence against my client, only snippets of him heading home and donning gloves – perhaps merely an act to shield himself from the frigid weather. James Jones Senior is a compassionate and protective man. Who would do anything for Layla. He is not guilty. He should be granted his freedom, and your verdict should resound – not guilty."

Having concluded his closing statement, Foster returned to the table alongside James Senior, who managed to maintain a stoic exterior, though adrenaline surged through his veins at the prospect of potential freedom and the unsettling question of whether he might escape the consequences of a heinous crime.

The judge adjourned the proceedings, urging the jury to rest well and emphasising the gravity of their role in the case. The next time they reconvened in the courtroom would determine whether James Senior would be declared guilty or not guilty.

The Smith family were overwhelmed with distress and anger. Foster's assertion that a "not guilty" verdict would be the best course for Layla and her family starkly contrasted their own beliefs, leaving them in vehement disagreement.

In the midst of it all, Officer Bellis spotted Luton and beckoned him to join him in the car for a private conversation. Their last interaction before the courtroom had been when they had framed James Junior and Luton had purposefully omitted any mention of the messages he had sent to Alfie. He intended to keep it that way.

Bellis began to discuss his plan concerning James Junior, but he faced a significant predicament – there was no longer a plan. He needed Luton's assistance.

"Listen, mate, we're in this together. I don't appreciate you causing trouble with me in public."

Luton's face was unchanged.

"I need a favour, and it's related to our previous involvement in framing James," Bellis says, as he starts glancing out the window, wary of prying eyes.

"I've done my part, and I don't want any more to do with it," Luton replied, visibly uncomfortable in the car.

Officer Bellis adopted a more assertive tone. "I've made it clear what could happen if you don't help me. If you value your freedom, you'll cooperate."

Luton reluctantly acknowledged the reality that he was ensnared in this with Bellis. He felt trapped.

"You know Alfie, right? I saw you talking with him once after the court trial last time," Bellis inquired.

"Sort of, but not really. Why?" Luton responded, his confusion evident. Telling another lie to Bellis.

"I need him," Bellis stated, a glint of excitement in his eyes as he relished the prospect of leveraging his badge's power.

"I believe I can get him on our side and ensure that James Junior ends up behind bars, just like his father will be."

Luton understood that his last message to Alfie had created a situation where he couldn't let him team up with Bellis. However, he had no clue about Alfie's current whereabouts, leaving him in a difficult predicament.

Upon returning home from the court, Oliver found his girlfriend, Freya, diligently cleaning the already immaculate kitchen. Her face lit up as he called out to her.

"I'm home, gorgeous," he announced, and she eagerly rushed over to envelop him in a warm embrace.

"So, how was your day out with your friends?" Freya inquired.

Unbeknownst to her, Oliver had been lying. During his purported outings with friends, he had actually been closely monitoring the trial. Ever since the news had broken, he had become fixated on it.

His former high school acquaintance, whom he had grown to despise, had now transformed into a notorious villain known worldwide.

Oliver stayed up late into the night, poring over details of the case, determined to keep Freya from getting too involved due to her inquisitive nature. His obsession with James Senior ran deep, motivating him to fabricate a profession. In reality, Oliver was not a therapist; he was a scientist. His wealth came from inventing a device that facilitated plant healing. While some fellow scientists regarded him as a lucky amateur, he remained indifferent to their opinions.

The reason for impersonating a therapist stemmed from his obsession with James Senior. He yearned to access the intimate details of the case for his personal amusement, which had led him to offer his card to Junior on the bus.

With such an elaborate web of deception, one could only speculate about the extent of his falsehoods. Oliver joined the ranks of those with motives to be the enigmatic Onyx, among many others. The Onyx remained at large, showing no signs of relenting.

CHAPTER 22

James Junior was just searching through the fridge, looking for his favourite snack. But then the situation took a bizarre turn.

He spotted a figure in the darkness that bore an uncanny resemblance to the Onyx. They were wearing feminine trainers, which led Junior to believe it may be a woman.

He rubbed his eyes in disbelief, double-checking what he had just witnessed from his hotel window. Was the Onyx planning another attack? Concern welled up inside him, but he remained torn between the desire to protect his family and the uncertainty of chasing after the potentially dangerous figure.

Finally, he mustered the courage to leave the hotel and pursue the Onyx. What did he have to lose? He had declared his intention to safeguard his family, even if it meant confronting the last evil within it.

The Onyx led Junior through winding and eerie routes in the town, traversing graveyards and derelict factories. Fear gnawed at James; this individual had proven their willingness to kill without remorse in the past.

As they turned a corner, Junior realised it was a dead-end, an opportunity to wait for them to retrace their steps and make his move. This, however, was a precarious moment for him. Although the police had grown quieter and lacked further evidence to accuse him of being the Onyx, he remained in the spotlight. But now, the time had come to unveil the true identity of the Onyx, even if it meant risking his life.

The Onyx continued to move swiftly, completely unaware of James Junior's presence, as they were about to turn in the opposite direction from where he lay in wait. Junior had to act quickly. With a decisive throw, he sent a stone crashing into an empty water bottle on the ground, creating a loud noise that instantly drew the Onyx's attention. They altered their course, heading directly toward him.

As the Onyx closed in, Junior sprang into action, launching himself at them and forcefully slamming them into a nearby car. The impact triggered the car alarm, blaring loudly into the night. On the ground, a fierce struggle ensued, with the Onyx displaying surprising strength. Junior found himself overpowered and was tossed aside. He was surprised by the strength of the Onyx.

Now, for the first time, Junior laid eyes on the person behind the Onyx mask. The identity that had eluded him for so long was finally unveiled, and the realisation hit him like a tidal wave of emotion. It was his sister, Shannon, who had been the Emberglade murderer all along.

Shannon locked eyes with Junior as she stood over him. He lay there, wracked with pain and shock that the person beneath the Onyx mask had been his own flesh and blood. In the moments that followed, Shannon made a fateful decision to flee, disappearing into the night.

But Junior knew it couldn't end there. He was determined to uncover why Shannon had been out there and where she was headed. Resolving to investigate, he followed the path she had taken, which led to an old road flanked by abandoned factories.

The warehouses loomed on either side, most of them locked up tight, but one particular warehouse emitted strange sounds. Junior was almost certain he heard someone cry out for help, a plea for assistance. It seemed impossible that someone could still be alive in these forsaken buildings.

The door to the warehouse was securely locked, and Junior attempted to kick it down without success. It couldn't be that difficult. The door was already worn and deteriorated, he thought.

In a desperate moment, he spotted a massive log nearby, something he could barely lift. Determination filled him as he positioned himself at a distance from the door and charged at it with the log. With a resounding "bang," the door gave way and crashed to the floor, allowing him entry.

What Junior encountered inside left him in a state of despair. A lifeless body lay before him, a sight that, while not unfamiliar, was never easy to confront. But a few feet away from the corpse was a man, trapped in a cage, barely able to stand. He appeared to have been left there for days, deprived of food and water. Junior recognised him as Alfie, the man who had initiated the mob against his family. It was a moment of reckoning for James, torn between a desire for revenge and a moral imperative to help.

As he gazed upon Alfie, his weakened state stirred sympathy within him. Junior couldn't help but feel for him in this dire condition. He gently inquired,

"Who did this to you?" Junior asked.

However, Alfie's response was feeble, and he struggled to form coherent words, overcome by exhaustion and dehydration. With a weary shrug of his shoulders, he conveyed his helplessness. It was clear that the Onyx had been responsible for this torment, the sole name synonymous with trouble in the town.

I was desperate to find a key that might unlock Alfie's cage. I searched the immediate surroundings, but there were no signs of it. My only viable option remained summoning the police, although I harboured reservations about doing so, particularly if Officer Bellis were to arrive on the scene.

Restlessly, I waited for the police to arrive, unable to bear the sight of one lifeless body and another barely clinging to life.

When the police did arrive, Bellis was among them, but fortunately, he was accompanied by two other officers. The shocking tableau that greeted them in the warehouse left them stunned, the overpowering odour of death permeating the air with Joel's lifeless form beside Alfie.

I had already informed them about the cage over the phone, so they had brought substantial tools to facilitate its removal. Alfie was finally liberated from his cage, but he appeared reluctant to leave. Leaving the confines of that building meant he would never see his brother again.

The police carefully extricated him from the cage, and they tended to the remains of the deceased. Alfie, though feeble, mustered a weak protest, urging the officers to be gentle with him and Joel. He was swiftly transported to the hospital for immediate medical attention.

I remained behind to answer the police's inquiries. It was a difficult decision whether to disclose Shannon's identity as the Onyx. She was family, and we had shared a lifetime of memories together. It felt agonising to potentially expose her to the consequences of her actions, so I chose to keep that secret to myself, at least for the time being.

I recounted the events to the police, explaining that I had been out for a jog and had heard cries for help. With a touch of humour, I added,

"Luckily, my AirPods weren't charged." I half-expected the officers to leap to conclusions and suspect me once again, but to my surprise, they didn't.

Perhaps they had finally come to realise that I wasn't the Onyx. However, I couldn't shake the feeling that Bellis still harboured suspicions about me. He seemed like a different person when in the company of his colleagues compared to when he was alone. There was an underlying agenda there, and I could sense it.

Meanwhile, Alfie had been provided with some much-needed sustenance at the hospital, and he shared his harrowing ordeal with the police. He explained how he ended up in that cage and even showed them the exchange of text messages. Unfortunately, they were unable to trace the origin of the phone used for the messages. The Onyx remained elusive, cunning, and determined to continue their reign of terror.

CHAPTER 23

Officer Bellis returned home after Alfie's recent plea, claiming that it was James Junior who had saved his life, making it increasingly challenging to pin the murder on James. The question lingered: why did Bellis harbour such a deep-seated animosity toward James?

His career had always been in law enforcement, initially spent in a serene, affluent town where trouble was a rarity. However, his life took a dramatic turn when he was inexplicably transferred to Emberglade. Rumours circulated, suggesting that Bellis had been involved in an affair with a fellow police officer who subsequently turned out to be corrupt, aiding criminals for personal gain. It was even rumoured that Bellis might have been complicit but had managed to evade capture.

After his relocation to Emberglade, Bellis found himself in a tough spot. He couldn't trust anyone within the police department, and he was now stationed in one of the roughest and most perilous areas in the United Kingdom. He believed that if he could crack the Onyx case, he might secure a ticket back to the upscale town he once patrolled. That's why he was willing to manipulate evidence to frame the Jones family – it appeared to be a more plausible scenario. As long as he could convict someone deemed to be the Onyx in the public eye, it was a win for him.

Faced with his own personal and professional challenges, Bellis decided to meet up with Luton, despite growing doubts about Luton's true intentions. They rendezvoused outside a coffee shop, but Luton arrived late, testing Bellis's patience. However, Bellis recognised that Luton was his only option for assistance in the murky waters of Emberglade.

Luton arrived a frustrating thirty minutes late to their meeting, prompting Bellis to reprimand him.

"What time do you call this?" Bellis exclaimed.

"I've been busy, I'm sorry. I'm here now, aren't I?" Luton retorted, his tone defensive.

Bellis demanded an explanation for the lack of progress on their plan to recruit Alfie. Testing Luton's loyalty.

Luton, trying to cover his tracks, replied,

"Yes, I saw him yesterday. I told him the whole situation, and he told me to piss off. I don't think we can trust him." He fabricated a scenario, hoping to deceive Bellis.

However, Bellis instantly recognised the lie. He knew that Alfie had been trapped in the warehouse during the time Luton claimed to have received a reply.

Fury filled Bellis's eyes, and he seized Luton by the back of the neck, pulling him in close.

"I'm this close to pinning it all on you," he threatened, slamming Luton's head onto the table.

Luton winced in pain, then stood up, warning Bellis that he could turn the tables on him. But no one in the vicinity paid them any attention, and Luton stormed off, leaving Bellis frustrated and shouting for him to return.

With Luton no longer cooperating, Bellis decided it was time for Plan B. If Luton wouldn't help, he would frame Luton as the Onyx instead.

Bellis wasted no time and headed to the police station, where he encountered Officer Humphries, his partner throughout the case.

"Alright, officer, I've got an idea of who killed Joel, in fact, I know exactly who it is," Bellis said, wearing a sly smile. However, Officer Humphries did not share his enthusiasm.

"Have you not heard? You're off the case. We're sick of you trying to be a detective instead of doing simple police work," Humphries responded, seemingly relieved to have Bellis removed from the investigation, especially since they believed James Junior to be innocent.

Bellis couldn't shake the feeling of betrayal as the case he had poured so much effort into was abruptly taken away from him. He struggled to accept the news and attempted to argue his case, but his words fell on deaf ears. He was forcefully removed from the investigation.

Despite this setback, Bellis remained determined to ruin James Junior's life and be seen as the hero. He believed he didn't need the help of his fellow officers.

With his own plans still intact, Bellis had one more person he hoped to bring to his side: Oliver.

Dressed in plain civilian clothing, a white top, and brown trousers, Bellis arrived at Oliver's building. Oliver, viewing the security camera feed, was puzzled by Bellis's uncharacteristic appearance and demeanour. He sensed that something was amiss but allowed Bellis to enter his home, pressing the button to grant him access. They met in the fake therapy room, which Oliver had now transformed into an office-like space.

"What brings you here, Officer Bellis?" Oliver inquired, his confusion evident.

"You can call me Bellis. I have a proposal for you," Bellis responded, attempting to convey kindness and gentleness.

Oliver, however, was well aware of Bellis's reputation and found his behaviour quite unusual. Nevertheless, he reciprocated the kindness by offering Bellis a beverage, to which he accepted a cup of coffee.

They engaged in ordinary conversation, with Bellis carefully probing to gauge whether he could trust Oliver with the sensitive information he possessed.

He knew that Luton's opinion wouldn't carry much weight with the police, given his current circumstances. However, if Oliver were to cooperate, it could jeopardise his career or even lead to his arrest, a fact that weighed heavily on his mind.

Bellis asked Oliver for directions to the restroom and started walking in that direction. He glanced back to ensure he wasn't being watched, and as he turned the corner, he saw that Oliver was preoccupied making the coffee and not paying attention. This was his opportunity. He quickly changed directions and entered the adjacent room, filled with scientific equipment where Oliver conducted experiments.

As he began rifling through drawers, Bellis couldn't believe what he was finding. Notes meticulously detailing the daily routines of the people in Emberglade, including specific times for James Junior's departures from his hotel, his breakfast spot, and other potential locations he might visit. The notes contained information on every single resident of Emberglade.

His discovery took a darker turn as he uncovered strands of hair, a broken pair of glasses, and a bloodstained T-shirt—all pointing to the murders committed by the Onyx.

Bellis had stumbled upon the identity of the elusive killer, but it sent a chill of fear down his spine. He was now in the same room where these gruesome items were hidden, and the thought of getting caught terrified him. The realisation that he might be murdered for discovering this evidence began to haunt him.

Bellis returned to the room where Oliver was finishing his cup of coffee, but Oliver could tell that something was amiss. Bellis appeared pale, with a look of sheer terror in his eyes.

A sense of foreboding washed over Oliver as he walked over to the science room and noticed one of the drawers in his room was left slightly ajar. Panic gripped him, realising that an officer had seen the items he had kept as mementos from his murders. In a rush of anxiety, Oliver hurried back to his office, but Bellis was no longer there.

Bellis had already bolted from Oliver's house, his heart pounding with fear for his life. He held in his possession the most valuable piece of information in Emberglade—the identity of the Onyx. Meanwhile, James Junior believed it was Shannon, but he couldn't have been more wrong.

Oliver dashed out of his building, his sole focus on stopping Bellis from reaching anyone and revealing what he had discovered in his home. Desperation fuelled his pursuit, and he couldn't afford to let Bellis escape.

Bellis had a stocky build that hindered his speed, while Oliver was agile and swift. Closing the gap between them.

Their chase brought them near the untreated river, a place of cultural significance in the town, but one tainted by murky waters. Bellis attempted to cross the river to reach safety, but Oliver was an adept swimmer as well. He closed in on Bellis as they emerged from the river, and with determination in his eyes, Oliver grabbed a hefty rock. In a swift, brutal motion, he smashed the rock against the side of Bellis's head. Bellis dropped to the ground, a massive, immediate gash forming on his temple.

The Onyx was poised to commit yet another murder. He raised the bloodied rock and brought it down onto Bellis's skull two more times, ensuring a gruesome and deadly outcome. It was a brutal murder of a police officer, executed with ruthless precision, leaving behind no traces of the killer's identity. Oliver kept the murder weapon, then heaved the lifeless body into the filthy river, hoping that no one would venture into its waters and discover the concealed remains. The Emberglade murder, shrouded in secrecy, remained undisclosed to the world.

CHAPTER 24

Shockwaves erupt - Officer Bellis is missing, they assume he stormed out of Emberglade as he was taken off the Onyx case.

The Onyx remains at large, now brazenly targeting those meant to protect the town.

Terry and his vengeful mob want to continue their crusade but dare not risk the streets with tensions so high. Many feel only a guilty verdict for James Senior, pinning the killings on him, can restore order.

With his trial conclusion looming, an uneasy silence descends on the barricaded streets. Backup officers arrive, though some bitterly note this should have happened sooner.

Behind closed doors, fear and suspicion fester.

James replays his violent encounter with the masked attacker he believes to be the Onyx. In truth, it was his own sister Shannon who tackled him that night.

Racked with guilt, Shannon tries urgently to contact James and come clean. But he refuses her calls, their trust shattered. She longs to explain why she was out there, to clear this mess up. But James remains unreachable, withdrawn from the family.

Not long ago, the Joneses were a happy, tight-knit family who felt like best friends. Now James Senior's actions have splintered them apart. The warmth and laughter were replaced by isolation and secrets.

Shannon nearly gives up on reconnecting with her brother. But deep down, she clings to hope. However damaged, they are still family. With patience and honesty, even the most broken bonds can mend in time. When this nightmare finally ends, Shannon vows to make things right between them all.

Amidst the chaos, Shannon had started dating Devin. Their mother worried it was unhealthy and unfair to Devin to begin a relationship now. What were his intentions, courting the daughter of an accused murderer?

But Shannon had no time for Devin with urgency consuming her. She had to find James before he said something damning about her being the "Onyx." She was just trying to sneak out to go to Devins home. Her panicked attack on him was an unforgivably stupid mistake.

Sweet Selena offered to search with Shannon. After tracking Junior's phone to a remote mountain cliff, cold fear gripped them. Was he simply clearing his head, or poised to end it all?

They spotted Junior standing at the precipice and screamed, but he was oblivious. The only way to reach him was climbing the steep mountain, which could take twenty agonising minutes. They had to hurry before it was too late.

Adrenaline surging, the sisters scrambled up the rocky slope. Far above, James lingered at the edge, swarmed by dark thoughts. He felt infected by murderous family genes, worried he too could become capable of evil.

The stress and confusion of recent horrors had driven him to this cliff, contemplating ending the suffering forever. Taking deep breaths, he steeled himself to jump as Shannon and Selena climbed desperately.

Nearly spent, the sisters struggled onward. James' life hung agonisingly in the balance. If they didn't make it in time, he could be gone in an instant.

Thirty painstaking minutes crept by as they neared the mountain's peak, but they found themselves dreadfully behind schedule—ten minutes late to be precise. Despite putting forth their best efforts, the challenging weather conditions and their low fitness levels made their ascent much more difficult.

Upon finally reaching the summit, they spotted James, who was still seated near the precipice. Shannon's voice echoed through the chilly air, shattering the eerie silence. James, unaware of their approach, jumped in surprise. Seeing Shannon face-to-face again quickened his heart rate.

"James, what are you doing?" Shannon cried out, attempting to close the emotional distance between them.

In response, he urged Selena, his younger sister, to keep her distance.

"Get away from me, Shannon. Selena, you have to go. Don't trust her!" he implored, his desperation palpable. However, Selena disregarded his warning, her voice trembling with fear.

"It's not true, James. Please, just come over here. I'm worried," she pleaded, her breathless words revealing her anxiety.

"Worried? The entire town is concerned about us, Selena. Our whole family. They want us dead—all thanks to Dad and Shannon," he responded bitterly, his anger simmering just beneath the surface.

"James, it's not what it seemed like. I was sneaking off to see my boyfriend. The entire family knows about it now. But I promise! I didn't want them to worry about me being around a man," Shannon explained, hoping that her words would break through to him.

James remained resolute in his scepticism. He rose to his feet and peered over the edge once more. Selena made one final, heartfelt plea, fully aware of the urgency of the situation.

"Think about Mum, James, please. Yes, our lives are a mess, and I acknowledge that. But we have to protect Mum. If you do this, you'll be killing her!" Her words struck a chord with Junior, reminding him of his core mission: protecting his family. Even if Shannon were the murderer, his love for Selena and his mother was sufficient reason to go on.

He stepped back from the precipice and approached his sisters. Selena rushed over to embrace him tightly, while Shannon, still uncertain about her place in the unfolding drama, observed. As James drew nearer, Shannon was left uncertain of how to respond.

"Just tell me, Shannon, was it you? Please, be honest with me right now," he implored, his emotions laid bare. Overwhelmed with emotion, Shannon tearfully assured him that she was not the culprit. Finally relenting, James embraced her.

"I believe you, I don't know why, but I do," he admitted, finally letting go of the notion that his sister could be the murderer.

The Jones family was reunited, stronger than ever, ready to confront the challenges that lay ahead. When they awoke the next day, they would head to court to learn whether their father, James Senior, had indeed committed the murder of Layla Smith.

CHAPTER 25

The atmosphere in Emberglade was palpable, with the entire community on edge as they anxiously awaited the trial's outcome. The tension was thick as the Jones and Smith families made their way to the courthouse. Upon their arrival, they were met with a throng of news reporters and social media influencers, all eager to pose probing questions about their emotions.

As the Jones family navigated through the sea of reporters, Shannon, unable to contain her frustration any longer, lashed out in response to the hurtful questions hurled their way.

"Just leave us alone!" she snapped, pushing one persistent reporter who inadvertently dropped their camera in the process. The enraged reporter shouted in anger, vowing to exact revenge with words.

The Smith family, opting for a more composed approach, kept their heads down and ignored the reporters' provocations.

Inside the courtroom, nerves were running high, intensifying with each passing minute. Both families clung to their hopes, praying fervently that the verdict would favour their side.

James Senior, exuding an air of confidence, made his way to the courtroom entrance. He briefly acknowledged his family with a subtle, reassuring smile and a wink, silently conveying his longing to be reunited with them. However, he was well aware that if their efforts failed, he could be facing a lengthy prison sentence.

With the closing statements concluded, both sides had said their piece, leaving no further room for persuasion before the judge or jury. The fate of the families now rested solely on the verdict that the jury would deliver. As they gathered, they couldn't help but feel sympathy for both families, yet they understood that their decision had to be based on the evidence and the law, rather than emotions.

The Judge presided firmly, prepared to deliver the momentous verdict on James Senior.'s fate.

"Will the defendant please rise," the Judge requested.

James stood up, his confidence slightly waning as he understood that this one sentence would determine his future. In the back of the courtroom, Oliver observed the proceedings, relishing every moment of the Jones family's anguish.

"I hereby announce my verdict," declared the Judge.

James glanced toward the jury, seeking some form of solace as the verdict was being delivered. Darius Smith had his hands covering his face, unable to watch due to the overwhelming emotional toll. Finally, the Judge provided the answer they all awaited.

"The court finds the defendant guilty of intentional murder in the first degree," the Judge pronounced.

The courtroom erupted into a cacophony of cheers and applause. The Smith family had achieved the justice they sought for Layla. James Senior would be confined to prison for a substantial period.

"The defendant is hereby sentenced to a term of Thirty years, to be served at Emberglade prison. This sentence includes no possibility of parole."

This trial became the most significant event in Emberglade's history, thrusting the town into the global spotlight, whether for better or worse.

The Jones family found themselves shattered, losing the hope they clung to since the case first made headlines. The hope that their father was innocent was now cruelly snatched away, leaving a void in their lives.

Their mother, attending the trial for the first time, deeply regretted it. She was in denial, refusing to accept that a man she had once been married to could be capable of committing murder with his own hands. They all wondered how they would be treated in the public eye from now on.

News of the verdict spread throughout the community, and the town celebrated it as a personal victory. The only obstacle that remained to restore harmony in the town was capturing the Onyx.

The police believed they had uncovered some evidence that might lead them to the elusive criminal.

The police had access to technology that could track a person's phone, but there was a significant problem. The Onyx used a burner phone, and no one knew the details except for one officer. This officer managed to send the burner phone number to Officer Humphries via email, but it was cleverly encoded to ensure the Onyx wouldn't discover the transmission. The officer who sent this information was Officer Bellis.

Bellis, driven by his experience and determination, had encountered the evidence in Oliver's room. He had to document it but also spotted the burner phone. It was then that he sent the encoded email while fleeing from Oliver's home, fully aware that he might not escape him.

The police arrived unannounced at Oliver's home, banging and ringing to no avail. Finally they broke in, scouring for evidence. His science room seemed suspicious but was empty. They were about to give up, until they checked under the sink and discovered strands of hair and a bracelet engraved "LS" - Layla's initials. How did he acquire this? Did he kill her too? Was the first thoughts of officer Humphries.

It seemed impossible, but a darker story was taking shape...

Back when Emberglade was a peaceful town, James Senior raced to the hospital in a panic, clinging to the slim hope that doctors could somehow revive Layla's lifeless body from the night before, the strangulation. But how did she die?

After James Junior left the pub, an old friend approached James Senior - Oliver. Without introduction, he showed James a photo of Layla in bed with Alfie, obtained by hacking Alfie's phone. Oliver knew this would enrage the jealous James.

When James Senior questioned the photo's authenticity, Oliver seemed sympathetic. But his true aim was pushing James to lash out violently at Layla that night.

Oliver harboured deep resentment toward them both - Layla for leaving him and James for being her new lover and ex friend.

That night, an intoxicated James stumbled home in the biting cold and donned his usual gloves. Seeing Layla triggered the image of her with Alfie, igniting a blind rage. He savagely strangled her, only stopping when realisation hit. But his mercurial mood swings resumed, and a darker impulse took over.

James's assumption that Layla was dead proved to be gravely mistaken.

Moments later, Layla's body stirred, snapping back to life. While it took her a few minutes to regain her breath, she struggled to get up for another agonising ten minutes.

During this time, Oliver had been lurking outside, an unseen witness to the disturbing scene that unfolded inside the house. Overwhelmed by guilt and emotional turmoil, James sought refuge in the bathroom, gazing at his own tear-streaked reflection, haunted by the heinous actions he had just committed.

Meanwhile, Oliver, driven by a sinister desire for revenge, clandestinely broke into the house and grappled with Layla, wrestling her to the ground. With a chilling smile on his face, he resumed the chokehold, determined to extinguish her life.

"If I can't have you, no one can." Oliver whispered.

After swiftly accomplishing his grim task, he exited the premises, leaving behind the lifeless body for James to discover upon his return.

Oliver derived a perverse thrill from exacting revenge, and this malevolent desire only intensified. As a scientist, he possessed the knowledge and skill to meticulously erase any traces of his DNA and navigate the labyrinth of security cameras in Emberglade.

His insatiable lust for vengeance drove him to commit his second murder—a brutal assault on James Senior's sister, aimed at shattering the lives of those James held dear. In his relentless pursuit of causing suffering, he plunged a blade into her spine, depriving her of life unfairly, just as he believed he had been wronged.

For his third victim, Oliver embarked on an elaborate scheme. He meticulously tracked the daily routines of Emberglade's residents, patiently awaiting the perfect moment to strike. Positioned at a corner shop, he targeted James's ex-girlfriend, selecting her as the easiest prey due to her solitary lifestyle and regular visits to the store. Though his original plan went awry, forcing him to employ a brick from the ground, he executed the murder with chilling precision, leaving behind no trace of his DNA.

Regrettably, when Bellis uncovered his true identity, Oliver felt compelled to take the officer's life as well, eliminating a threat to his secret. These ruthless acts of violence unfolded in the shadowy depths of Emberglade, where James Senior languished in prison, bearing the weight of innocence in a world filled with darkness.

CHAPTER 26

The Emberglade Police continued their relentless search for the elusive Onyx, now suspecting that Oliver was the culprit behind the series of crimes.

Officer Bellis had tragically sacrificed his life in the pursuit of justice, leaving Officer Humphries with a heavy burden of guilt for the sour note on which their last encounter had ended. He had removed him from the case, a decision that weighed on him heavily. However, he remained determined to honour Bellis by resolving the case.

The police meticulously examined the items seized from Oliver's house, hoping to extract valuable DNA evidence. Their efforts bore fruit as they identified Oliver's DNA among the prints, further cementing their suspicion of him. Oliver made the mistake of not removing the DNA, from touching the weapons after it was cleaned.

Although they had deployed hundreds of officers throughout the town, Oliver had managed to elude them, leading authorities to believe that he had fled Emberglade.

The police clung to a glimmer of hope that Oliver still possessed the burner phone, unaware that its number had been compromised, allowing them to track its location.

Humphries received the vital information he had been waiting for, pinpointing the phone's whereabouts on a remote farm on the outskirts of Emberglade. This farm, with its vast, private land and isolation from neighbouring houses, served as Oliver's sanctuary, a place where he could find safety and seclusion, essentially his secret backup hideaway, beyond anyone's suspicion.

Little did Oliver know that the police had him cornered, closing in on his exact location. At the farm, he and his girlfriend were meticulously erasing any traces of their presence, aiming to leave no evidence behind. Not wanting the police or anyone to know this is their home. Oliver had no choice but to tell his beloved girlfriend he was the Onyx. Who was foolish and still wanted to protect her lover.

They displayed certain items from their victims, with Officer Bellis's police hat standing out prominently.

This inadvertent error would provide additional evidence linking Oliver to the murders. Oliver's girlfriend, once a close friend of Layla, had harboured anger towards the Jones family following Layla's tragic death.

Oliver had used her for her intelligence, as he believed it would aid his murderous plans. He told her about the murders of James Senior's family but no mention of Layla's murder..

As the police arrived at the farm, they faced a formidable obstacle—a massive fence that blocked their way. They wasted no time and sounded the buzzer, announcing their presence.

"Oliver, this is the Emberglade Police. If you don't open this gate, we will force our way in."

The realisation that the police had located his hidden farm hit Oliver like a wave of panic. He scrambled for an escape plan, rushing to the back where his car was parked. However, escaping without encountering the police seemed impossible.

The police successfully breached the fence using the tools they had brought with them. They had arrived in force, fully aware of the dangerous nature of the man they were pursuing. Their determination was unwavering, and they were resolute in their mission to arrest him.

James monitored his security cameras, observing as the police officers disembarked from their vehicles. Realising that the authorities were closing in, he made a frantic decision to escape.

He jumped in his car and floored the accelerator, leaving his girlfriend alone in the house, feeling betrayed and frightened. Oliver's car careened around the corner, coming face to face with the officers who had tried to return to their vehicles.

With reckless speed, Oliver tore across the once-pristine grass of his farm. The officers managed to block his escape routes, but he showed no signs of slowing down. He aimed his vehicle directly at an officer, hurtling toward them at a terrifying One hundred and ten miles per hour.

At the last moment, the officer managed to leap out of harm's way. Oliver, believing he had eluded capture, failed to notice the spike strip lying ahead.

The encounter with the spike strip sent his car into a chaotic spin, and it ultimately flipped over into a thicket, crashing down with brutal force. The impact caused Oliver's head to slam backward in the violent crash.

Police officers had a mix of relief and concern, watching as their tactic succeeded, but they worried about the injuries Oliver might have sustained. Despite the heinous crimes he had committed, they held fast to their commitment to protect Emberglade's community members. They rushed to the overturned vehicle, which now emitted a plume of smoke.

Carefully, they inspected the wreckage and found Oliver still alive inside the car, but in excruciating pain and struggling to move. With great care, they extricated him from the wreckage and immediately transported him to the hospital.

Once he had sufficiently recovered, they would proceed with his arrest, and the elusive Emberglade murderer, the Onyx, had finally been captured.

News of James Senior's guilty verdict had already brought some relief to the town, but the revelation that the true Onyx had been apprehended was met with widespread joy and celebration.

Emberglade was swiftly returning to its former joyful, close-knit community.

Residents congratulated each other for their collective strength and resilience throughout the ordeal. Even the Jones family, previously treated with suspicion, now received the town's love and sympathy as it became clear that the real killer had been at large, targeting their family under the influence of the man now behind bars.

The Jones family had become recognisable figures, not just in Emberglade but around the world. Their experiences had thrust Emberglade onto the global map. This newfound fame transformed them from being perceived as villains into beloved local celebrities.

James Junior made the decision to leave his job, instead opting to share his story and experiences, earning him substantial fees for speaking engagements. He spoke passionately about the trials he endured, including being falsely accused of murder multiple times, all while maintaining his resilience and strength.

Selena found a job at the local cinema, a place that brought her immense happiness. For her, it was the perfect environment to be in.

Tessa, their mother, took some time off from work and revealed the newfound love and support from the community. She resumed her weekend tradition of bowling with a renewed sense of joy.

Shannon, meanwhile, finally achieved her dream of becoming an actor. The spotlight that had been thrust upon her family also cast her in its glow, garnering her the attention she needed to launch her career as a reality TV star.

The town basked in a renewed spirit of unity and safety, grateful for the return of peace and harmony. However, a lingering question remained: how long would this tranquillity last? Would the truth about James Senior.l eventually emerge? And, sadly, would this town witness another tragic murder in its midst?

Printed in Great Britain
by Amazon

5cc694e1-a848-4ca3-92f7-6a7264c10c38R01